"Since we're s

Roc began politely, "y
share the captain's qu
aboard to discover what's going on here, didn't you? What better way—"

He shouldn't have been surprised when the bottle of fine Caribbean rum came flying his way. Thankfully he was quick. He closed the door, then heard the bottle smash against it.

There had been a time when he hadn't thought Melinda tough at all. There had been a time when those eyes had lit on his with sea-green passion, when the golden threads of her hair had curled over the bronze of his chest, tangled in his fingers. When those perfect legs had entwined with his own.

There had been a time. But that had been long ago. And now there was only one thing he could do....

Dear Reader:

*We at Silhouette are very excited to bring you this reading **Sensation**. Look out for the four books which appear in our Silhouette **Sensation** series every month. These stories will have the high quality you have come to expect from Silhouette, and their varied and provocative plots will encourage you to explore the wonder of falling in love – again and again!*

Emotions run high in these drama-filled novels. Greater sensual detail and an extra edge of realism intensify the hero and heroine's relationship so that you cannot help but be caught up in their every change of mood.

*We hope you enjoy this **Sensation** – and will go on to enjoy many more.*

We would love to hear your comments and encourage you to write to us:

Jane Nicholls
Silhouette Books
PO Box 236
Thornton Road
Croydon
Surrey
CR9 3RU

Between Roc and a Hard Place

HEATHER GRAHAM POZZESSERE

DID YOU PURCHASE THIS BOOK WITHOUT A COVER?
If you did, you should be aware it is **stolen property** as it was reported *unsold and destroyed* by a retailer. Neither the author nor the publisher has received any payment for this book.

All the characters in this book have no existence outside the imagination of the author, and have no relation whatsoever to anyone bearing the same name or names. They are not even distantly inspired by any individual known or unknown to the author, and all the incidents are pure invention.

First published in Great Britain in 1995
by Silhouette Books, Eton House, 18-24 Paradise Road,
Richmond, Surrey TW9 1SR

ISBN 0 373 59536 0

18-9503

Printed in Great Britain by
BPC Paperbacks Ltd

Other novels by Heather Graham Pozzessere

Silhouette Sensation

Night Moves
Double Entendre
A Matter of Circumstance
Bride of the Tiger
All in the Family
King of the Castle
Strangers in Paradise
Angel of Mercy
This Rough Magic
Lucia in Love
Borrowed Angel
A Perilous Eden
Forever My Love
Wedding Bell Blues
Snowfire
Hatfield and McCoy

Silhouette Special Edition

The Game of Love

Silhouette Christmas Stories 1993
"The Christmas Bride"

Worldwide Books
"The di Medici Bride"

To Doreen and John and Baby Westermark,
with lots of love and best wishes.

Chapter 1

"Captain! We've caught more than fish in the net, sir!"

Roc Trellyn strode forward on the deck of the *Crystal Lee,* his bare feet silent against the wooden planking. They were between the Florida peninsula and the Bahamas, the weather was warm and balmy, and he was clad in nothing but a faded pair of blue cutoffs. As befit a man who spent the majority of his life on the water, his bare chest and arms were deeply bronzed; even the dark hair on his chest was bleached until the tips were golden.

He was a tall man, lean, hard and well muscled, a swimmer, a diver, a sailor. He was dark, with jet black hair, a little shaggy since they had been at sea for several weeks now, and his face was just as bronzed as his shoulders. His features were striking, saved from true handsomeness by the rugged edges brought on by constant exposure to the sea and sun. His cheekbones were high, his nose straight, his mouth broad and generous, sensual. Against the utter darkness of his face, however, his eyes were a brilliant, steely blue. He was a man it was impossible not to notice.

"Captain!" The call came again even as he reached the pile of netting and fish on the forward deck of the *Crystal Lee.* It was Bruce Willowby who seemed so concerned, his first mate on this and most cruises, his best friend on and off the ship, though his entire crew was small and close-knit. Bruce and he had majored in marine biology together at the University of Miami, and ever since, they had cast their fates to the wind together. Bruce was tall, lean, with sun-bleached white-blond hair, also shaggy now, and almond-shaped dark eyes.

The entire crew of the *Crystal Lee* had gathered around the netting, alerted by Bruce's calls. Connie, Bruce's sister, their best cook and a skilled diver, was standing by his side. Connie was a pretty woman, with her brother's platinum hair and beautiful dark eyes. Then there was Peter Castro, half Cuban, half Irish-American, dark and green-eyed, small and wiry, a whiz with sonar equipment. Completing the crew were Joe and Marina Tobago, husband and wife, Bahamians, and two of the best divers and swimmers he had come across in all his life. When they had spare time in the evenings, Roc liked to race Joe Tobago. Sometimes he won. A lot of the time he lost. And Joe would tell him in his melodic singsong that he was getting old and letting himself go slack. That, of course, always spurred him on, and he usually won the next race. He wasn't slipping all that badly, he would assure Joe in return.

Except that maybe he was.

Hell, he had to be.

Because Bruce was right. He had just hauled up a hell of a lot more than fish.

Something, no some*one*, was struggling in the netting. Oddly, the entire crew had stepped back. It was their surprise, he was certain, that had caused them to do so.

He stood dead still himself, at first. Then he realized not just what but *who* he had caught. She hadn't seen him yet.

He stepped back, moving to stand on the first of the steps leading to the helm, out of the woman's line of vision, and motioned to Bruce, who lifted a curious brow at him. He waved a hand, indicating that they should release her from the netting, though it would be a grudging effort on his part.

Bruce shrugged, then lifted the netting that had entangled the woman.

And from his vantage point, Roc saw her. Really saw her.

A silent whistle echoed in his head.

She hadn't changed.

Just what had he pulled up from the ocean's depths? A ghost from the past? A siren from the sea?

She was kneeling on the deck, so he couldn't really see her height or size, but he didn't need to. She was tall and slim and elegantly, sensually built. Her hair was dripping wet, plastered against her face and head, so he couldn't really judge its color now. It didn't matter. He already knew it. When that hair dried, it would be the color of sunlight. Not pale, but golden, with specks of red fire.

She was still the most exquisite creature he had ever seen.

Her face was lifted as she stared at Bruce. It was stunning in its perfection. Her cheeks were high and classical, her nose small and straight, her lips richly defined, rose-colored against the elegant tan of her flesh. Her face was a perfect oval, her eyes very large and wide-set, framed by high brows and velvet lashes. He could see the color of her eyes clearly, furious and flashing, an aquamarine to rival the most glorious waters of the Caribbean.

He'd seen them flash that way before.

This time, however, her angry stare was directed at Bruce; she seemed to have taken him as the one in charge.

She pointed a finger at him. "You, sir, should be arrested and put under lock and key! How dare you!"

Bruce stepped back in surprise. He had obviously been taken in by her heart-stopping beauty. Poor Bruce. Ah, well, he was a big boy. And he had realized that Roc had recognized her. In a few minutes, he might put two and two together himself.

"Lady, you're in our net—" he began.

"Exactly! I'm in your net!"

Bruce—ever the gentleman—moved to try to help her up.

She didn't want help. She shoved his hand aside, struggling on her own power.

Ah, and there she was, at her full height, all five feet eight inches of her.

A sudden pang swept mercilessly through Roc's heart. *No, she hadn't changed.* She was still perfect. And it wasn't because she was clad so scantily; her bathing suit was actually a rather subdued one. It was a black one-piece, low-cut in the back to her waist, with French-cut thighs.

It was the way she wore what she wore.

She was slim, but extremely shapely. Her legs were long and finely muscled, her waist very slim, her hips just perfectly flared, her breasts just perfectly...

Perfect.

Roc crossed his arms over his chest, surveying her as she surveyed Bruce.

Despite her startling beauty, he sure as hell didn't need this. He was having enough trouble with his latest venture without adding a problem like this. She was a pain. And she was trouble. Definitely trouble.

A niggling suspicion tore at his mind. Had she been sent to spy on him? To see just what he was up to with the *Crystal Lee?*

His eyes roamed up and down her. She *was* perfect—perfect bait. As stunning as ever a silver fish was as it wriggled on a hook, a lure to bring in the big catch...

Bruce was still staring at her. Just staring. Roc was tempted to walk over and snap his friend's gaping mouth shut, but he didn't want her seeing him, not yet, so he resisted the temptation.

"Oh!" she cried aloud in exasperation, the fury flashing even more brightly in her eyes. "What in God's name is the matter with you? How can you be so entirely careless?"

Bruce found his voice at last. "Lady, what are you talking about? I can't even figure out where you came from! We're moving in deep waters. We're not in swimming or diving areas, we're—"

"The type of fishing you're doing kills hundreds of marine mammals yearly!"

"I've never caught a marine mammal in my life!" Bruce assured her quickly.

"You've just caught me!" she exclaimed. "And I'm just about the same size as a small dolphin."

Oh, lord. So she was supposed to be a bleeding-heart liberal, or something of the sort.

Was it true?

Roc doubted it.

Oh, not that she didn't care about the dolphins. She did. She loved the water, almost as passionately as he did. Maybe more so.

But had she come here because of the dolphins?

No. He was absolutely sure of that.

And he *had* caught a marine mammal—when he wasn't even a fisherman.

But she knew that. She just didn't know yet that this was his ship. That he was captaining the voyage.

She was here to discover just what he—or the *Crystal Lee*—was up to. Well, maybe, he thought grimly, just maybe, she was going to get her chance to find out.

Bruce was looking over her head now, to the helm. Roc made another motion. Bruce stared at him, confused for a moment. Then he shrugged. Roc was obviously up to something.

Suddenly Bruce smiled.

Roc wondered if his friend had just figured out who their beautiful mermaid was.

"Ma'am, if you have a problem with us, you'll have to take it up with the captain."

Ah, there they went, those perfect brows of hers, flying up in surprise.

"You're not the captain?" she said to Bruce.

He shook his head.

"Then take me to him—immediately."

"Ah, I don't think he's quite ready to receive company yet. Maybe you'd like a cup of coffee or tea, or a soda? Even a beer?"

"I don't want anything to drink, thank you. I just want to see the captain, have my say and get back to civilization!"

"We are civilized here, miss . . . ?" Connie murmured with a sniff.

She glanced at Connie. "I'm sorry," she said quickly. "I'd just really like to speak to the captain and get back." She flashed them all a beautiful smile. Ah, here it came, the charm. "I really am sorry. I was just so frightened. If I've been rude to you all, I didn't mean to be. It's your captain with whom I have a fierce disagreement."

She didn't yet know just how fierce! Roc thought.

Then he decided it was time to disappear into the captain's cabin. The *Crystal Lee* wasn't all that big—it was going to be difficult finding privacy, but he meant to have a little of it.

Silently, he turned, padding across the decking to the large cabin in the far aft of the ship. He could hear the others talking as he quietly opened the door and slipped into the cabin. "You come, missy," Marina Tobago was saying, slipping a chestnut arm around her shoulders. "I make the most wonderful coffee in the entire world. It will make everything look a little better."

Marina was going to take her into the galley and central living quarters. Fine. All the sonar and other special equipment was below deck, wedged in between the crew quarters. Space was of necessity tight on the *Crystal Lee,* but she was a beautifully built vessel, so well designed that Joe and Marina had their cabin, Connie had her own smaller place, and Peter and Bruce shared the larger living quarters just beneath Roc's captain's quarters.

He sat behind the antique ship's desk he had managed to procure for the *Crystal Lee.* Damn. He was still amazed. How could *she* be here? Maybe he shouldn't have been so amazed. She was, after all, her father's daughter.

And it still seemed that his heart was being squeezed, just a little.

No, a lot...

How long had it been?

Nearly three years. She hadn't changed.

Had he?

Sometimes it had felt as if she had aged him an entire decade....

Maybe several.

He reached absently into his bottom drawer. There was a bottle of special dark Caribbean rum there. He didn't open it often. Not on a trip like this one.

Tonight...

Tonight he needed a drink.

He set the bottle on his desk and reached for a tumbler, then discarded the idea and took a long swig out of the bottle. Whew. It burned. Hot and sweet, going down. Warmed his heart. Melted away the pain.

No, not really.

There was a quick tap on his door. Bruce entered. His eyes were wide, his manner excited.

"I've got it!" he said. "It's her! Right? Ms. Melinda Davenport. I can't believe I didn't see it right away, except that in most of the pictures, she's *dry*. She does look a little different, soaking wet and all. Damn, I'm sorry. I didn't mean to be so slow-witted!"

Roc shook his head. "Bruce, you weren't slow-witted. How could you have been expected to know? I almost stepped on her before I realized it myself."

Bruce shook his head. "God, but she's beautiful!"

Roc nodded wryly, then looked meaningfully at Bruce. "But watch it. She's treacherous. Cunning. Don't forget, she's old man Davenport's daughter. She can be vicious. Hard as nails. Tough as leather. As charming as formaldehyde!"

Bruce grinned. "She sounds like the Wicked Witch of the West."

"And don't you forget it!"

"Want to get her off the ship fast, huh?" Bruce said.

Roc leaned forward, grinning. "Not on your life!" he exclaimed softly. "Hey, the way I see it, this was no accident. She wanted to come aboard. Well, she's here now. She can just stay a while."

Bruce frowned. "Won't that be kidnapping?"

"She came aboard my boat."

"Well, we did pull her up in a net."

"And she slipped herself into that net on purpose, I assure you."

"Sounds like you really dislike her!"

"She's absolute trouble," he promised.

Bruce shook his head again sorrowfully. Then he arched a brow. "By the way—did you ever actually get a divorce from her?"

Roc started.

Had he?

No, actually, he hadn't done anything. But surely she had. Old man Davenport would have seen to that! Roc was always at sea. He'd never been served any papers, but then, he wouldn't have been around to receive them. The way things had ended had been so furious and wild....

"Wouldn't that be something?" he murmured.

"What?"

He grinned. "If our little imposter is still my wife!"

Bruce smiled in return. "Well, it might help out in case of a kidnapping charge!"

Roc sat back, remembering his brief and stormy marriage. The wildness, the fights... the lovemaking.

A searing jolt seemed to rip right through his body. He gritted his teeth, leaning back again, and swallowed another long draft of good Caribbean rum.

"Why don't you bring the lady in?" he suggested. "The captain is ready to be met."

Bruce flashed him a quick salute and hurried out. A second later, the cabin door opened and she came on in.

Melinda. Melly...

She was drying, and drying nicely. Connie had supplied her with clothes, white baggy pants and a white tailored shirt with short sleeves. The tails were tied at her waist in a knot.

Her hair was drying. Long, wavy, spilling golden over her shoulders. She wore no makeup at all. Melinda had no need for it.

She strode in, already having taken a deep breath and ready to vent her anger on the captain.

But even as she stepped in, he was rising. And before she could speak, he was smiling, greeting her smoothly.

"My, my. *Ms.* Davenport. To what do we owe this very strange, er, pleasure?"

The air rushed out of her. Aquamarine eyes lit on him, amazed.

But was she as amazed as she seemed? He doubted it.

"You!" she breathed.

He arched one dark brow. "These are my waters," he reminded her politely. "They always have been."

Her lips seemed to be trembling slightly. But was it for real?

He lifted a hand. "Do come in, Ms. Davenport." He paused, cocking his head, staring at her. "It is *Ms.* Davenport, isn't it? You did divorce me, I assume?"

And then he knew. Instantly.

She paled to the color of snow.

She had never divorced him.

She had probably just assumed that he had divorced her, the way he had assumed . . .

Oh, no. This was rich! Really, really rich!

He started to laugh, the sound deep and husky in the small room. "So it isn't Ms. Davenport! What a startling surprise. Almost as surprising as pulling one's ex-wife up in a fishing net at sea. Except you're not my ex-wife."

"And you're not a fisherman!" she lashed out, at last finding breath again.

"Right," he said, his laughter having faded, his voice tense. He set his hands on the table, leaning across it as he demanded, "So just what are you doing on my vessel, Melinda?"

"I was caught just like a dolphin because of your absolute carelessness—"

"Wrong!"

"Damn you!" she cried, striding across the room, ready to accost him—until she realized just how close she had come.

Close enough to touch.

He could see the pulse beating at the base of her throat. The rise and fall of her breasts. Just as she could see the ripple of his naked chest with every breath of air he took.

She shook her head, the movement a little wild. And just a little . . . desperate.

Melinda, beautiful in white, golden hair cascading over her shoulders, aquamarine eyes a damp, gemstone fire. Chin held high. Always held so high.

"You're not going to believe a word I say to you, no matter what. So why don't we end this impossible situation right here and now?"

He sat back in his chair, controlling the wild rush of emotions surging through him. "This impossible situation?"

"Me. Here."

He shook his head, as if trying to understand her better. "Melinda, you connived your way aboard my vessel."

"I was caught up in your—"

"No, Melinda, I don't think so."

"How can you not think so? I was in your net—"

"Yes, but I think you ended up there on purpose."

"You would!" she cried. "You would never credit such a thing to your own inability—"

"Ah. And it just happened to be *my* boat you came upon, eh?"

"What does it matter?" she cried. "Just take me to port. Any port! Then this will all be over and done."

He smiled at her. Just as pleasantly as he could manage.

"But I'm not ready to head in to port."

"I am."

He rose again, striding around the desk, pausing just before her. His smile deepened. "But I'm the captain, Ms. Davenport. And what I say goes."

He walked past her, heading for the door.

"You can't possibly mean to keep me a prisoner on this boat!" she cried.

"Prisoner!" he exclaimed, swinging around. "Oh, you are mistaken!"

"Then you will take me to port—"

"Sorry!" he informed her. "But please, think of yourself as a guest, not as a prisoner!"

"You son of a—" she called after him.

He closed the door on the last word, then leaned against it, smiling. But it was a painful smile. Then he turned back, opened the door, and grinned.

"Since we are still married," he offered politely, "you're more than welcome to share the captain's quarters. I mean, you did come aboard to discover just what's going on here, didn't you? What better way to make discoveries?"

He knew her. He knew her well. So he shouldn't have been surprised when the bottle of fine Caribbean rum came flying his way.

Thankfully, he was quick.

He closed the door, then heard the bottle clank against it.

Once again, he smiled.

The bottle hadn't broken.

But then his smile faded. The rum hadn't eased a thing. He seemed to be burning inside and out. Giant fingers had closed around his heart.

There had been a time when he hadn't thought her tough at all. And never had he seen her as a witch.

There had been a time when those eyes had lit on his with sea-green passion, when the golden threads of her hair had curled over the bronze of his chest, tangled in his fingers. When those perfect legs had entwined with his own. When they had lain beneath the stars, feeling the swell of the sea beneath them, dreaming...

There had been a time.

But that had been long ago now.

And though she might still be his wife, she was definitely old man Davenport's daughter.

And she had come here to spy; of that he was convinced.

And there was only one thing he could do. He had to make damned sure that she didn't return with any information whatsoever.

And there was only one way to do that. He had to make sure she didn't return. Not until he had made his claim.

However long that took.

Melinda . . . Aboard this boat. Day after day.

Torture!

He gritted his teeth. All right. So torture it would be. But he was going to make damned certain that it was torture for both of them!

Chapter 2

He was gone.

Melinda sank into the chair behind the captain's desk and realized that she was shaking. She gripped her fingers together, trying to stop.

So, this was his boat! She should have known, she had suspected, but still, she hadn't really been prepared....

With a soft groan she let her head fall to the desk. She had wanted it to be his boat. Face it, she had wanted this to be his boat, even if she actually *was* spying in a way. This time, if she could, she would make sure that things went the way they should have gone before. She owed him that much.

Was that *really* why she was here? she mocked herself.

Wasn't she still just a bit...a little bit...in love with him?

Not that it mattered. They might still be married—and that was truly a shock!—but the way he had looked at her had clearly indicated that he felt he had brought a shark on board.

Her fingers were starting to tremble again. Well, what had she expected? That he would welcome her with open arms after what she had done?

On the other hand, he was the one who had walked out.

After she had taken her father's side. Against him, against her husband, and even Jonathan Davenport admitted now that he had been wrong, that he should have given credit where credit had been due....

It was all so long ago.

But she'd never managed to convince herself that it was over, she realized. She'd been so naive, so foolish—and so wrong in so many ways. She could clearly remember her fury that he could say anything ill about her father. In fact, she could remember how angry they had both been, the words that had flown, the accusations, the recriminations. Then she could remember being in his arms, believing that he had listened to her, that he had understood, that everything would be all right. She could remember the tempest and the sweetness of making love....

And she could very clearly remember not believing that he was really leaving when he walked away the next morning. He had asked her to come, of course. She just hadn't believed that he would really go.

And she hadn't seen him since.

At first she'd thought he hadn't changed, but now she knew he had. He was three years older, wiser, determined, confident and very set in his ways. His hair was a little shaggy; he wasn't getting it cut very often. He had probably decided that he just didn't have the time. If he was on a quest . . .

He was definitely on a quest. Her father had said that if anyone could find the *Contessa Maria,* it would be Roc Trellyn. Of course, Jonathan was looking for the ship, but he hadn't been the one to plant the idea of trying to find out if Roc was in pursuit of the elusive galleon and, if so, how he was doing. It was Eric who had rather offhandedly given her the idea one night when they had all been in that little pub in Key West.

"There's no doubt Trellyn will be after this one. He's always been convinced that the *Contessa* went down between Florida and the Bahamas, no matter how the scholars have insisted that she went down closer to Cuba. This new evidence must have him dancing for joy. I'll bet he's out there right now, in one of those supposed *fishing* boats, searching his little heart out. Oh, to be a fly on that boat! But then again, Melinda, you could just ask your ex what he knows and what he's up to!"

He'd given her one of his lazy half smiles. Eric was very good at lazy half smiles.

She admitted that he was an attractive man, tall, blond, tan, lithe and muscled, and charming in his own way. He worked with her father on and off, moaned and drank beer with her father on and off. She'd tried to like him, tried to date him, and sometimes she'd even enjoyed herself. But she'd kept her distance from him, all the same. They'd danced, they'd kissed—but she'd managed to stay out of bed with him and still retain the friendship or flirtation or whatever it was. She had created the distance, though she hadn't really known why. Or else she'd never admitted why until now.

It all came back to Roc.

He wasn't Roc.

No one was. She'd learned that painfully in all the long and lonely nights since he had left. She had never known, never imagined, the torture of lying alone at night, remembering him, the hard-muscled length of his body, the whisper of his breath, the excitement of his touch, the magic of his kiss. The simple sweetness of falling asleep in his arms, of dreaming there, of awakening to find herself still held so tenderly.

Her fingers started shaking again despite her efforts to still them. His passions always ran so deep. He had loved the sea, the water, diving, the hunt, the adventure.

And once upon a time he had loved her. She had lost that. And she could probably never have it back. It had been a mistake to come, and she should leave as quickly as possible. She had to get away from him. It hurt more to be near him than it did to be away. She had betrayed him. Once he had loved her so deeply, but now he seemed to despise her with the same fierce energy. She couldn't let herself dream about what had been....

Because it was gone. All gone. All that remained was the look he had given her tonight. As if she were a cobra with a forked tongue.

She shivered suddenly, looking around the cabin. Was she locked in here? He had said that he wouldn't take her to port, so what did he mean to do with her?

Maybe he was waiting for her to go to him, to beg for mercy.

Never! She hadn't completely lost her pride.

And her fingers were still shaking. She didn't really know him anymore. Didn't know his heart or his feelings—or if he was sleeping with the very pretty blond woman she had seen on deck.

So what should she do?

Wait. She just had to wait. Eventually he would come back. He had to, didn't he?

"So that's Melinda Davenport," Bruce said, shaking his head. He'd been standing by the port side railing when Roc came slamming out of his cabin.

Roc breathed deeply, studying his first mate, determined not to reveal the turmoil of his emotions to anyone, especially his best friend.

"Trellyn," he said softly.

"Trellyn?" Bruce's eyebrows shot up.

Roc shrugged. "It seems she never divorced me."

"Oh. Well, surely you two can rectify that. Next time we pull into Fort Lauderdale or Miami, you can see an attorney."

"Right," Roc agreed. He walked to the rail, his fingers curling around the polished wood as he looked out to sea.

He should head for port right now. Get her off the boat. The *Crystal Lee*'s sixty feet didn't provide enough room for the two of them to be together.

"She must be spying for her father," Bruce surmised.

"Must be."

"So, we get rid of her quickly, right?"

"We should."

"But we don't?"

Roc spun around and leaned against the rail, crossing his arms over his chest. He was definitely feeling a little malicious. "She wanted to come aboard. We'll keep her aboard for a while."

Bruce shook his head. "You're the captain."

"Right."

"She is Davenport's daughter."

"Right. But she's on *my* boat. And, startling as it seems, she's still *my* wife."

"You mean that you're still in—"

"I'm not still anything," he said impatiently. "But I'm not sailing into any port, either. We were scheduled to dive tomorrow—we'll dive."

Connie came around the corner, looking at them both with grave concern. "So you do know her?" she asked Roc.

"Know her?" Bruce snorted. "Inside and out!"

"She's my ex-wife," Roc told Connie.

"Only she isn't his ex anymore," Bruce said, shaking his head worriedly again.

"How can you suddenly undo being an ex?" Connie asked.

Peter Castro came around the corner next. "You get married again," he told Connie. He looked at Roc. "*¿Que pasa, Capitano?*"

"You married her again already?" Connie asked, totally confused.

Bruce gave her an amused look. "Connie, don't be so dense. He never divorced her. She never divorced him. And neither one of them ever stays on land long enough to read a newspaper or collect the mail, so they both assumed they were divorced."

"Davenport's daughter!" Peter said with a soft whistle. "Well, she's spying. She has to be."

"We have to get rid of her," Connie said.

"He doesn't want to," Bruce said mournfully.

"But she's obviously come to see where you're searching! She'll go back and tell her father, and they'll both be after the *Contessa Maria* right where we're looking," Connie told Roc, her brows furrowed.

"Don't let her take you for a ride, my friend," Peter warned him.

Roc sighed, irritated. "She isn't taking me anywhere. And she isn't going to tell her father anything, because I'm not letting her go back to him until after I've made my claim."

Connie gasped. "Can we keep her that long? Isn't that kidnapping?"

"She did come aboard voluntarily, right?" Roc said.

"Well, technically, we did haul her up in a fishing net," Bruce reminded him.

Suddenly Roc smelled smoke. The others smelled it at the same time. "Dinner!" Connie cried. "Oh, no! Marina asked me to watch the potatoes!" She whirled around, running down the deck to hurry down the stairs to reach the galley.

"I think," Roc said, "that dinner seems to be more than ready. We should go eat."

"But what about . . . your wife?" Bruce asked him.

"She's not locked in. If she's hungry, she'll find her way to the galley."

"She could find her way to a lot of other places."

"Not with all of us up and ready to stop her."

"Are we staying up all night?"

"I'll see that she doesn't go where she shouldn't," Roc said softly.

"Oh," Bruce murmured. "Oh . . ."

"No *oh!*" Roc said wearily. "I'll just be keeping my eye on her."

"Be careful now."

"She's five feet eight and maybe a hundred and thirty pounds. I've got five inches and eighty pounds on her. I'll be all right."

"Right. And fire coral looks delicate and beautiful, but touch it, and you've got one hell of a burn!"

"Bruce! I left the lady, remember? I'll be all right." He refrained from mentioning that it had half killed him to do so and only his pride had kept him from going back to her.

He should just have dragged her along. After all, he was bigger, as he had told Bruce.

He might have carried her away. . . .

But he couldn't have changed things. No amount of anger or muscle could have swayed her from her father.

Bruce studied him and grinned. "Well, I wouldn't be all right if she were in *my* cabin. I would never sleep. I'd sit there all night and—ouch!" He broke off as Peter's elbow connected with his ribs. "Hey!"

"She's his ex-wife, not yours!" Peter reminded him pointedly.

"Not an *ex,* remember?" Bruce insisted in return.

Roc let out a groan of exasperation. "She may not be an ex, but my days with the Davenports are long over. Let's have dinner."

"Without her? We're really going to let her starve?" Bruce asked unhappily.

"It's my guess she'll come prowling out in a few minutes. It will be hard for her to do much spying if she just hides out in my cabin, right?"

Bruce shrugged.

"Let's go."

In the galley, Roc sat at the big boothlike table that ran down half the port side length of the combined galley and dining room and found Marina Tobago staring at him with her dark, soulful eyes as she set bowls of potatoes and vegetables and plates of grilled grouper on the table. He smiled as he sat, and didn't say anything. Peter slid in near Roc. Connie set the salad on the table and sat down, too. Bruce cleared his throat and took a seat opposite Roc. Joe Tobago, tall, burned bronze, sat down next to Bruce. "Eh, Captain. Roc, my friend!" he said softly, his Bahamian singsong accent pleasant and melodious. "Just what do we say if this mermaid from the sea talks to us?"

It was finally too much. Roc started to laugh. "I don't know. It depends on what she says. Joe, if she wants to discuss the weather, discuss it. If she asks how you cook your grouper, Marina, just go ahead and tell her. If she wants to know anything about our boat or our search for the *Contessa,* tell her that she has to come to me. If she offers to help with the dishes, let her!"

Marina grinned. "Davenport's daughter does the dishes?"

"She's very good aboard a boat," Roc said, the words softer than he had intended. But she *was* good. Melinda loved the water. She loved the reefs, loved snorkling and diving for treasure. She could handle herself in any motorboat or sailboat; she loved to fish—and she had never shirked a bit of the cleanup in anything. He supposed he had to credit Davenport for that. Despite their differences, there were many things Roc had admired about the man. He didn't have a prejudiced bone in his body; he judged both men and women on their abilities. He demanded as much from himself as he had asked from any of his crew, and if he had ever been more demanding of anyone, it had been Melinda. In many ways, she was like her father. She loved adventure, loved people and was always intrigued by anything new and different. She would taste any dish of food, dive into any treasure hunt—just as she had dived into his net!

He shrugged, still determined to give no hint of emotion. "She knows what she's doing. If she gets in your way, just put her to work."

"We're diving tomorrow, though," Connie said worriedly. "We haven't come up with anything but that old World War Two hunk on the sonar. Nothing to prove. But still, she's going to know where you go in, and if we find anything..." Connie trailed off and paused a minute. "Well, her father was awfully quick to steal a find from you once before!"

"I told you, we don't let her go until the claim is made," Roc reminded her.

"And how do we manage that? Sit on her? At some point we're going to have to make port for supplies!"

"I'll handle things!" he said softly.

Marina sniffed audibly. The table fell silent. "Who's going down tomorrow?" Peter asked.

"Marina and Joe can stay aboard, the rest of us will dive. Then Connie and Bruce can stay aboard the next day, and I hope we'll have something to show for our efforts soon."

"You're still convinced we're looking in the right place?" Joe asked.

"More convinced than ever," Roc said firmly.

"Roc," Joe said softly, leaning forward with a piece of fish speared on his fork. "I trust your judgment, but why can't we find anything with the sonar equipment?"

Roc shrugged, stretching across the table to pour iced tea into his glass. He had nearly grabbed one of the icy beers in front of him, but he had already swallowed a fair amount of rum—instant reaction to Melinda. He wanted his wits about him for the rest of the night.

"I've always been convinced that the *Contessa* went down here. Everything I've found convinces me that they were much farther north than the historians have argued when the storm first hit. Now those letters from that sailor to his sister have been uncovered, and he was convinced that they were farther north than their captain believed, and that's what he put in the letter. Anyway, I have a hunch. I had it the minute I first heard of the *Contessa.* She's within ten miles of us here, I swear it. And I'm going to find her."

"And everyone else in the world is going to be on top of us very soon, now that the letter's common knowledge," Bruce commented.

"Like our... guest," Connie said.

Roc smiled and looked at Marina, who had taken her place beside her husband. "If she does ask you about the grouper, make sure you tell her, OK? It's absolutely delicious, Marina."

"Thanks, Captain," Marina told him. Her eyes were still worried.

"Actually, I think she *should* do dishes, don't you?" he asked Marina.

"I don't mind—"

"Stowaways should work, so I've always thought."

"But," Connie reminded him, "she hasn't shown up to have dinner, so how can we make her wash the dishes?"

"Hmm. That is a dilemma," Roc agreed. "All right, well, we'll wait until she actually eats a meal to make her wash the dishes. How's that?"

"We'll see," Marina commented. She reached across the table and tapped his plate. "If it's so delicious, eat."

"Yes, ma'am!" Roc said, and speared a big bite of grouper. He chewed it, swallowed and smiled. "I'm eating!"

He finished his fish quickly, talked idly about the dive as he ate his salad, and then pushed the potatoes around on his plate—Connie had forgotten to keep her eye on them, and they did have a slightly burned taste. He drained his tea, then rose, thanking Marina again, repeating that the meal had been excellent. He set his dishes on the small counter by the small sink and very small dishwasher, then made his way up the steps to the main deck.

Well, Melinda hadn't appeared for dinner. Maybe she'd managed to carry a stash of candy bars in her bathing suit or something.

Maybe she was afraid of his crew.

No, not Melinda.

Maybe she hadn't been ready to face him again yet, and then again, maybe she had been waiting for an invitation, for him to come back, to beg her to forget his bad manners and please grace them all with her presence.

No way.

Pride must cometh before a fall, but it was a hell of a good thing to cling to. He wasn't begging Melinda Davenport—Trellyn—to do anything. Not again.

He had begged her once. He'd begged her to come with him. And either she hadn't believed that he would really go...

Or else she hadn't cared.

He leaned over the rail, looking out at the coming night. The sun had nearly set. The sea was dark, mysterious. The air was cool and light and refreshing on his cheeks. There were just the remnants of the sunset on the horizon, beautiful streaks of gold and red and rust. The anchor had been cast, and they were stationary, just rolling slightly on the gentle waves. It was a beautiful night, a spectacular one, really.

A lot like the first night he had seen her.

He'd had a month off from working for Davenport and had been working with Bruce and Connie on his own when he'd received a message from Davenport. He was ready to start up again, and if Roc could meet him in Largo on the following Friday, Davenport would appreciate it. He, Bruce and Connie had just finished bringing up the personal property of a Connecticut man whose yacht had gone down in the Florida Straits, so he wouldn't be leaving in the midst of anything, and working with Davenport was an incredible experience. He always learned something new.

In Largo, Jinks Smith, Davenport's cook and all-around man, came to pick him up in Davenport's dinghy. Davenport's boat was anchored just out of the harbor. Roc had climbed aboard, completely unaware that anything—everything—was about to change in his life. He was wearing cutoffs and sandals, and his gear was in a pile in front of him, when Davenport came out of the main cabin, greeting him with a warm handshake, telling him about the treasure they would be hunting for in the ensuing months.

Then he had met Melinda.

The sun had been like this. And she had been a dark silhouette against the blazing red horizon. All he had seen at first had been her lithe shape. She had been a shadow moving with sensual grace across the blood-red horizon, reaching her father, slipping her arms around him. Then she had been a shadow no longer. She was wearing a two-piece suit, a figure-hugging bikini. He could remember the color, brilliant aquamarine, like her eyes. She was exquisitely shaped. She'd just finished diving, he imagined, because her hair was still wet, only a few long strands dry and flying free to catch the dying sun.

And she was hugging Davenport....

A spiral of jealousy had curled into Roc's stomach almost instantaneously, since he hadn't known, at that first meeting, who she was. Jonathan Davenport was an even twenty years his daughter's senior, a man of forty-one that year, and as Roc knew that his employer had a daughter but had never seen her, he'd assumed that Melinda was the older man's latest fling. He had to admit being a little resentful that Jonathan could acquire such an elegant young creature.

But then Jonathan had quickly disentangled himself from her and introduced them. "Roc, meet my daughter, Melinda. She'll be with me from now on. Melly, Roc Trellyn. He's my right hand. You two be sure to get along with each other now."

She'd been right in front of him. Blue-green eyes, dazzling, her hair like endless waves of gold in the firelit sunset. He'd never been shy with the opposite sex; he'd had his share of relationships, and he'd imagined that at his age—twenty-eight, back then—his head controlled both his heart and his loins. He'd kept his affairs unemotional because he'd never met anyone who fascinated him more than the lure of the sea.

But that had been before Davenport's sea-siren daughter. His head hadn't had a chance against his heart and his loins.

She looked at him. Just like a princess from the sea.

Those aquamarine eyes touched his with instant challenge. She reached out a delicate, golden hand and touched his, then pulled quickly away. "How do you do, Mr. Trellyn."

Her voice was cool, completely disinterested. She turned back to her father, apparently annoyed that they were not alone. "I didn't realize you were busy, Father. I think I'll shower now. We can talk later, when you're not involved with the help."

If she'd slapped him, she couldn't have made her feelings any plainer.

In fact, come to think of it, he'd been itching to slap her back at the time.

However, he'd managed to keep his cool, though Davenport had been furious with her for her lack of manners. He'd apologized to Roc, explaining, "My ex-wife, her mother, was just killed in an accident. It's no excuse for her behavior, really. . . ." He shrugged. "I've had her with me often over the years, of course. She's a phenomenal diver, you'll see. She's out of college now, and she'll be with us full time."

Full time. Full torture.

Well, the sea siren had been nothing but a bitch to him, so at first he had managed to steer clear of her easily enough. She barely spoke to him, and when she did, it was in a condescending tone. But once, when they'd made port in Jamaica, he'd left the ship in a suit and tie, having met an old friend from his University of Miami days on the beach earlier and made plans to go out. He hadn't returned until the next morning. She had been helping Jinks serve breakfast, and his eggs had landed right on his lap.

"Sorry!" she told him.

What a lie! He'd leaped up, the hot food beginning to burn through his swim trunks.

"Let me cool you off."

And she had, dousing him with a pitcher of water.

Perhaps he'd lost it a little bit there. He'd gripped her by the upper arms and told her quite frankly that she was a spoiled little brat, and if she did something like that to him again, he would damned well see that she had a burning rear end.

She turned the color of flame, wrenched free from him and disappeared. Jinks had been there, but it seemed he never said anything to Davenport about the incident.

And neither did Melinda.

Two days later they clashed again. Melinda had gone down to a wreck and stayed too long. The others had been concentrating on a map. Roc—who, despite himself, always had half an eye on her—was aware that her tanks held only thirty minutes of air.

He went down quickly himself, only to find her trying to free a gold chain from some twisted metal. He caught her hand, and she spun on him, shocked, furious. He pointed to her watch, and she wrenched free, clearly furious with him.

And then her air gave out. She began to struggle, and he forced her to share his air. Finally, slowly, once she calmed down, he led them to the surface.

Well, needless to say, she hadn't thanked him. She was furious and convinced that, if he'd just left her alone, she could have surfaced on her own.

He could have throttled her then and there, but instead he somehow managed to swim away.

And he still kept quiet to her father.

Then, after the next day, it didn't really matter, because that was the day they came into Bimini and stayed at the huge hotel by the casino. He'd taken his key from the desk and gone up to his room to start putting his things away. But when he went to put his shaving equipment in the bathroom, he found the shower occupied. Melinda was just stepping out of it, blond hair damp, curling slightly around the perfect oval of her face. His eyes, of course, didn't stay on her face. They fell. He felt the tension she always aroused in him tighten and spiral incredibly. Damn her. She was a witch. He couldn't begin to understand the attraction, and he forced his eyes back to hers.

She snatched up a towel. "How dare you?"

"Me!" he snapped. "I was given this room!"

"Well, I was given it, too, so you can just get out. Anyway, I don't believe you! How can you just stand there? My God, you did this on purpose—"

"Get off it, princess! I'd just as soon burst in on a barracuda!"

He'd managed to turn around and stride to the bedroom, gritting his teeth, feeling every muscle in his body clench with fury... and frustration.

But then something amazing happened. He heard his name spoken very softly.

"Roc?"

He turned. She was wrapped in a huge white towel, and she was staring at him, a liquid glimmer in her beautiful eyes.

"I'm—I'm sorry. I've been wretched to you since you came. I didn't mean to be, and I apologize. It's just that you're so close to my father, and I need him now, and I—" She paused, a bit of a smile curving her lips. "I was jealous."

His stomach knotted. She was beautiful and vulnerable and suddenly as soft as silk. He knew right then that he was in trouble. He should stay exactly where he was, tell her that he accepted her apology and that he was sorry about her mother, and then he should walk out as quickly as possible. If he didn't he would be trapped. For eternity. He would taste her sweet forbidden fruit and find himself hopelessly drugged on it.

But there were tears in her eyes. And he felt compelled to walk forward, compelled to take her into his arms. "I'm sorry," he heard himself saying very softly. "About your mother. You have behaved abominably, though, so I can't apologize for my own behavior.'' She almost smiled. His arm was around her, and somehow he swept her up to his lap, and she leaned against his shoulder. "Your father told me about your loss.''

"Did he tell you everything?'' she whispered. "That Mother was drunk? That she caused the accident?''

"No,'' he murmured.

Her pain seemed to streak through him. "I tried!" she whispered. "I tried for so many years! But she kept—drinking. I must not have been there enough. I must have been a rotten daughter—''

"Hey, hey! Stop that! Melinda, you can't blame yourself, and no one else can blame you, either. You have to be sorry, you have to miss her, but you have to remember that alcoholism is a disease!''

Her eyes looked into his, so naked, so vulnernable, so trusting. Then she was sobbing softly, and he found himself kissing those tears from her cheeks. "It's all right, it's all right. . . .''

Her arms were tight around his neck. The towel she was wearing was slipping away, and he was still clad in nothing but trunks and sandals, and the fiery pressure of her body was against his, her naked breasts a torment against his chest, the nipples so hard, tempting his flesh. Then his kiss found her lips, and she returned it passionately. Her mouth parted for his, and his tongue delved deeply into the sweetness of her. Deeply, deeply . . .

He was losing himself, and it didn't seem to matter. The towel was gone completely, having fallen somewhere, and they were stretched out on the soft, comforter-covered bed. She seemed to know exactly what she was doing, returning kiss for kiss, her fingers moving sensually over his shoulders and back. His kiss began to stray, finding the wonderful silken texture of her throat, closing over her breasts, tasting, taunting. She pressed against him, soft, sweet, yielding, so enticing, her body arching to his touch.

He was fascinated by the woman he held in his arms, tempted beyond measure. He couldn't taste enough of her as his lips and tongue traveled the length of her, resting intimately here and there. Her fingers remained upon him, her touch erotic, her cries compelling, her warmth exciting and inviting. She writhed, twisted, called his name. . . .

He could have drowned in her more swiftly than he would have been lost in any sea. The scent of her hair, of her flesh, drove him wild. Yet with all the hunger he was slow, wanting her to want him with the same fierce fever. And it seemed that she did.

He didn't take her until he couldn't bear the aching a minute longer. And when he did, he was stunned, but it was too late. He could have shot them both before he could have risen and left her. She was stiff, startled. She had known, of course, but perhaps she hadn't realized *exactly* what she would feel, or that something so incredibly sweet could suddenly be so incredibly painful. But she clung to him, gritting her teeth, and he whispered to her, softly, gently, kissing her, caressing her. And in time she was with him again, the anguish having ebbed, the fire having been lit once again. A blaze so fierce . . .

When it burst upon him, he felt almost as if he'd never made love before, it was so volatile, explosive, shattering, sweet, to be with her. Yet even as the sheen of heat cooled on his body, he was ready to kick himself. Davenport's daughter. He'd tried so damned hard . . .

Bull.

He'd wanted her, needed her, from the first moment she had moved so gracefully into his life. But she might have told him, warned him, said something. So he was a little bit angry with her, and when the wonder and excitement were gone, she got angry, too, telling him that she'd had the right to choose to be with him, the right to choose not to be with others.

"You don't owe me anything," she assured him, trying to drag the covers around herself. She could be so damned dignified when she chose.

"It's not a matter of owing!" he said angrily. "It's a matter of—"

Of what, he wasn't sure.

"You can't be afraid of my father!"

"Of course not!"

She swallowed hard, looking away. "I knew I wanted you!" she whispered very softly. "I was horrible because of it. The night you stayed out, I was so jealous, that was why I—"

"What?"

"Well, it was why I dumped the eggs on you. And the water, of course. I didn't want you—out with another woman."

He started to laugh then. Intrigued. And in a matter of minutes she was in his arms again, and the magic was still there, stronger, greater.

She didn't want to say anything to her father right away, so they didn't. But by the end of a week, the lying, the not speaking, bothered Roc. He told her that it was going to be all or nothing. He loved her, he believed that she loved him, and they were going to be married.

She had no argument with him. She smiled, her beautiful eyes so dazzling, and she leaped into his arms. In all of his life, he had never been so happy.

But things change. . . .

Leaning against the rail now, Roc realized that the sun had finally gone down. Stars were appearing. The night was blanketed by darkness, all color gone except for that spattering of stars.

"That was then and this is now!" he reminded himself.

He turned. The boat was quiet. He'd been standing at the rail forever, and they'd all let him be. There were no more sounds of clanking dishes, footfalls or conversation.

They'd all gone to bed, he surmised, leaving him to his thoughts.

So now what was he going to do? Bright guy. He had left Melinda in his cabin. There was a nice comfortable bed in there... with Melinda in it.

The thought made his pulse quicken, and he almost groaned aloud. Comfortable, all right. Sometimes he could forget the fights, but he had never managed to forget the feel of her at night, the silken softness of her flesh, the feel of her hair, long and lush and taunting against him. Her curves, her derriere thrust against him, the fullness of her breast in his hand...

Bright, bright boy. He'd even gone to college! Then he'd gone and stuck his ex-wife in his own comfortable cabin, where she was probably sleeping like a kitten while he stood out on deck in the middle of the night in torture.

No, she wasn't sleeping. Not like a kitten. Not at all.

From his position by the port side rail he could see the door to his cabin. Moving back a hair, he could still watch and yet be fairly certain that he couldn't be seen in turn.

Yes...

It was cracking open. The door to his cabin was cracking open.

And there was Melinda. Looking out carefully. Listening. She was very still for several long moments. Then she slipped into the pale starlight and paused, listening and waiting again.

She still looked like a sea sprite, slim and elegant, so innocent in white, that cloud of golden hair gleaming even in such dim lighting. Her delicate face turned, her head cocked. At last she seemed satisfied and headed for the stairway to the living cabin.

Slowly, silently, he followed her.

Was she hungry at last? Trying to raid the galley now, when the crew were resting?

No...

She was hungry, all right, he thought angrily. For information. Little witch! She was heading swiftly down the next ladder, down to the lowest deck.

Down to where they kept their sonar equipment.

He followed, still in silence. Waited until she stood right before the equipment, studying it, leaning closer to carefully view the screen.

He came up behind her, stopping just an inch away from touching her.

"Looking for something?" he whispered politely.

A gasp seemed to choke her. On instinct, she started to run.

On instinct, he went after her, catching her when she reached the ladder, pulling her down.

She lost her balance, and he lost his.

And they crashed together to the floor.

Chapter 3

Perhaps he should have felt some sympathy for her—despite his efforts to swing around as they fell, she hit the floor first, with him stretched out on top of her. And they landed hard, but she didn't cry out. She simply stared at him, furious and outraged, in the strange green light from the sonar equipment.

He should have felt some sympathy—except that she had been spying.

He didn't ease his weight completely off her, but he did slide to one side, resting an elbow comfortably on the floor while he smiled at her, his eyes slightly narrowed.

"Isn't this romantic?" he said softly.

Her teeth ground together audibly. "Romantic? You're breaking every bone in my body."

"Imagine. If you'd kept your bones where they should have been, they'd be in no danger of breakage now."

"Would you get off me, please?" Aquamarine eyes flashed with fury into his.

His smile deepened as the rest of his muscles stiffened. Maybe he should move. He could feel her warmth, each subtle shift of her body. As furious as he was, he still felt the urge to throttle her being overwhelmed by the urge to strip her then and there and make love to her by the ethereal green light.

"Spies have been hanged throughout the centuries, you know," he informed her politely. "Tortured, and then hanged. Or maybe shot."

"I wasn't spying."

"Oh, right. You were looking for the head."

Her eyes flashed again, and she shoved her hands against his chest. Determined, he didn't move.

"I could kick you!" she reminded him.

"I know," he replied. "Forewarned is forearmed." He shifted his weight over her body in such a way that she couldn't possibly move enough to do him any real harm.

"Roc—"

"Melinda."

She inhaled deeply, then exhaled on a long note of exasperation.

"You've been spying, Melinda."

"I was picked up in your net—"

"You swam into that net on purpose. You knew exactly what you were doing. You were fully aware that this boat was out here searching for the *Contessa,* and I'm willing to bet you even suspected it might be *my* boat. Of course, if it hadn't been, I can just imagine the sweet smiles and wide-eyed innocence you would have given the captain—any captain, from a toothless old salt to a green-behind-the-ears young lad. Then you would have set to until you knew exactly what the crew had discovered, at which point you would have brought all the news back to Papa. Of course—"

He broke off at her sudden flurry of motion, as he felt the sudden sting of pain and heard the crack of her palm against his cheek.

He stroked his cheek, his eyes on fire as he stared at her.

"Davenport must be getting pretty desperate!" he said softly. "He was willing just to drop you off in the middle of the ocean and assume that you'd make it safely aboard in a fishing net!"

She was aiming at him again; he knew it. This time he caught her hand before it could fly. There seemed to be a glistening of tears in her eyes when she retorted, "This has nothing to do with my father! He didn't let me out to swim into any fishing net!"

"Oh, Melinda! I know you're half fish, but don't expect me to believe that anyone just swam this far out—"

"I didn't say that! I said my father had nothing to do with this. It was my idea."

"To come spy?"

Every sleek muscle beneath him seemed to tighten. Once again, he could hear that furious grinding of her teeth.

"You're not going to have any canines left," he warned her. "And if I remember correctly—"

"I never bit you!" she lashed out.

"Well, we do have different memories of our relationship, don't we?" he asked politely.

She surged against him in a sudden, strong fury. She was very slim, but wiry, and she nearly toppled him.

Uh-uh. He wasn't moving.

"If you don't get off of me . . . !" she raged.

"What *are* you going to do?" he inquired. "Call Daddy?"

"Off!" she demanded, grasping the bare flesh of his arms, nails digging as she shoved at him.

He caught her wrists. Stared into her wild eyes. "How about asking politely?"

"You are a hateful human being."

"That's not asking anything, and it's not in the least polite."

"I'm warning you—"

"And I'm warning you, Melinda," he said impatiently. "This is my boat. You're a damned stowaway and spy, and I should have you arrested."

"I wasn't spying—"

"Well, there's a head in my cabin, and the galley is on the deck above us. What could you possibly be doing down here?"

"Looking for the radio," she said.

"Have to tell Daddy you're safe?" he asked.

She ignored that. "Would you *please* be so kind as to let me up?" she asked.

He thought that one over. Anger wasn't helping him. Maybe it was just making things worse. Being this close to her seemed to tie his muscles in knots, boil his blood and cause a definite rise in his libido.

He couldn't stay where he was much longer. Not unless he wanted her to know just how exactly and completely she was on his mind—and in his system.

"That was fairly polite," he acknowledged. He got swiftly to his feet and reached a hand down to her. She started to rise on her own, but he impatiently grasped hold of her wrist with a little growl and dragged her up. Maybe it was better; maybe it was worse. The twelve inches between them now didn't seem like much at all. He wasn't touching her, but his body could still feel the warmth where they had been touching. He was suddenly more aware of her sweet, clean scent. Connie's soap and talc, he thought, but scents were different on different women, and this was all Melinda.

"May I use the radio?" she asked.

"No. But I will radio your father for you."

He started to walk by her. Maybe she had miscalculated; the radio was at the helm. Or maybe she *hadn't* miscalculated. She had come down here to check out his progress before going to the radio.

"Roc, if you'll just let me call myself—"

"I told you, I'll do it."

"But I wasn't with my father!" she cried softly.

He had reached the first rung of the ladder, and he paused, hearing a note of desperation in her voice.

And also a note of the truth.

He stared at her.

"All right. So just who did drop you off in the middle of the ocean, assuming that you'd be picked up okay?"

She hesitated. "Does it really matter?" she finally asked softly. "If you'll just let me use the radio—"

"No, I just won't," he said flatly. He left the ladder and came back to stand before her. "Who were you with?"

"It's none—"

"Who?"

"Eric Longford," she said in a rush.

Longford.

Great waves of heat and fury suddenly came sweeping over him, like a massive tidal wave.

Longford.

He hated the man. Eric Longford was a tall, tanned beach bum, in Roc's opinion. He hadn't ever had two thoughts of his own, but he somehow managed to be in the right places with the right people at the right time to make a decent living from the sea. Roc and he had always been civil to one another in company, but the tension had always been there between them. Roc had always considered the man dangerous. The type to create huge waves right where the signs commanded *No Wake!* He was a careless diver, never gauging his time and oxygen. He was completely heedless of the delicate coral reefs around Florida and the Bahamas, casting anchor anywhere.

And worst of all, he was a womanizer who had always had his eye on Melinda, and Roc would have thought she had the good sense not to become involved with such a man.

"Eric Longford?" he repeated, trying to fight the fury that continued to wash over him. Had Longford already been in bed with his ex-wife?

No, not his ex. His *wife!*

He wanted to kill the man.

She must have seen it in his eyes, because she backed away from him. "It isn't what you think—" she began.

"How do you know what I think?" he grated out.

"Not that it matters!" she suddenly lashed back. "You walked out on me—"

"No, lady, I didn't walk out on you. You chose another man over me—it happened to be your father, but you made the choice just the same. And now—*Longford!*"

Her hands on her hips, she stood very tall and straight and regal and faced him. "You've been sailing around for three years now without the least concern for my welfare, and I'm sure you have no intention of giving me an accounting of how you spent your time. For the moment, you've chosen to keep me a prisoner on this boat. Therefore, you owe me the courtesy of letting me use your radio."

"I owe you the courtesy?" he exclaimed, his hand clenching into a fist. He raised it, swore suddenly, then turned around and slammed his hand into the wall.

His damned knuckles hurt like hell.

"Yeah, let's radio Longford!" he said. "The ass left you in the middle of the ocean, crawling into another man's net, but by all means, let's let him know that you're all right!"

"I told you," she said very softly, and there was a note of pleading in her voice, "this was *my* idea."

"Maybe I was off before. Way off. Your father would never have let you pull such a dangerous stunt!"

She backed away again. "Roc, please—"

"Is your father somewhere out there, too?" he asked her impatiently.

"I don't—"

"Bull! Is he out there?"

She turned away, glancing at the sonar screen. "I, er, I think so."

"Fine. We'll radio your father. He can call Longford if he wants."

He reached for her hand, unaware how angry he still was until she cried out at his touch. He forced himself to ease his hold on her.

"Come on!" he commanded.

"I am coming," she returned stiffly. "Where else would I be going?" she asked with aggravation. "And shush up, will you? I have a hardworking crew, and they're sleeping."

"You're the one who's shouting!"

Shouting. He wanted to shout. Scream. Tear his hair out. Tear *her* hair out. Smash Longford right in his tanned jaw.

He dragged her with him up to the living cabin, where she seemed to pull back.

Maybe she could catch the delicious aroma of dinner, still in the air.

Good. He hoped she was absolutely starving.

He pulled her out to the main deck, then directed her to the steps leading to the helm. She climbed as quickly as she could, all too aware of the angry man behind her.

He joined her a minute later, pushing her aside so he could take a seat in the captain's chair and pick up the mouthpiece for the radio. He switched it on, found his frequency and identified himself as the *Crystal Lee*. He stared at Melinda. "What's your father sailing on these days? I heard he just bought a new boat."

She was silent.

"Melinda."

She sighed. "I believe he's on the *Tiger Lilly*. But if you'd just let me do this myself—"

"I won't," he assured her. He flicked the radio on, identified himself once again and called the *Tiger Lilly*.

A few minutes later he heard Davenport's fuzzy voice. ''Roc?'' He sounded puzzled.

''Yes. I wanted to let you know I have something of yours. Over.''

There was silence, then static.

''Melinda? Is it Melinda? Over.''

''She'll be with me for a while. She's fine.''

He was startled when he *thought* he heard a sigh of relief. ''So she is with you. Over.''

''Yes. Over.''

He looked at Melinda, waiting for Davenport to make some protest, to tell him that he would be motoring his way over in the dead of night to pick up his daughter. Instead, Davenport sounded relieved.

''Melinda's alone? Over.''

''Yes. Over.''

Another sigh of relief. Roc sat back, staring at Melinda. She was very tall, straight, still. Staring at him with her blue-green eyes glittering, her chin high.

Then he realized something that almost made him smile. Davenport hated Longford almost as much as he did himself. Old man Davenport wasn't upset that Melinda was with him, because it meant she wasn't with Longford.

Longford . . .

Just thinking the name made his teeth grind together, his muscles tighten. He wanted to know just what she'd been doing with the man.

No, he didn't want to know.

Yes, he did. He wanted her to tell him that it had been entirely innocent!

"Melinda, what in God's name—" Davenport began suddenly, and if he hadn't been so angry himself, Roc might have found his old mentor's outburst amusing, just as it was amusing when Melinda snatched the hand-held mouthpiece and shouted quickly, "I'm a grown woman, Dad!"

She was still staring at Roc, who smiled. "Over," he said.

"What?"

"It's a radio communication. You should know that. Tell him 'over.'"

"Over!" she snapped.

There was still silence. Then some static. Then Davenport's voice, amused again. "You're after her, eh, Roc? Over."

"After her? Over."

"The *Contessa*. Over."

"Just searching around, like always. Over."

"Well, good luck, then. Until we meet again. Take care of her for me. Over."

Roc set the mouthpiece into its socket and studied Melinda. "Well, at least he isn't too concerned."

"If you'll excuse me," she said coolly, "it's very late."

Her chin high, nose in the air, she swung around like nobility to slide gracefully away.

He was still sitting in the broad captain's chair. So she thought she was about to disappear? Not on her life.

"Wait a minute!" He reached out, fingers curling around her wrist forcefully. "I did not excuse you!" With a flick of his arm, he dragged her back until she was directly in front of him, still standing, but between his knees.

"What now?" she enunciated crisply.

"I don't trust you, that's what. We'll go down together."

She lifted her arm, indicating the bronzed fingers that remained wound around her wrist. "I can only go so far, you know!"

He released her and stood so quickly that she jumped back, her temper growing.

"I already know you're carrying sonar equipment and that you're looking for the *Contessa!*" she exclaimed in exasperation. "And even if I weren't here and hadn't seen anything, it wouldn't have taken a genius to figure that out! You were the one who always insisted that the *Contessa* was out here, remember? All I've done—"

"Is come aboard to see if I've found her or not, and if so, get away fast enough to turn her over to your father—or Longford!"

"How dare you?" she demanded furiously.

He shrugged. "Mabye you're in business for yourself now."

He knew Melinda. He should have been prepared. Maybe he was prepared; maybe he just wanted her flying into his arms.

She did. Fists flailing, she was a whirlwind, striking out at him. He caught her quickly, crushing her against his body so she couldn't inflict any damage.

Her head fell back. Aquamarine eyes touched his, glistening.

Damage . . .

Without moving a finger, she could inflict it. And despite the torture, he was glad to hold her. Glad to feel her crushed against him.

"I'm not working for anyone!" She exclaimed angrily to him. "And if you weren't such a great ape—"

"You'd beat the truth into me?" he queried.

He was startled by the sudden passion in her voice. "Yes! Yes, that's exactly it. But you are an ape, and I'd appreciate it greatly if—"

"Longford?" he grated out suddenly.

"What difference does it make to you?" she cried in exasperation. "You walked away! You walked right out—"

"No, it wasn't exactly like that. Damn you, Melinda!"

"You left me!"

"No, you left me."

"I didn't move!"

He shook his head. "You didn't have to move. You left me. Geography had nothing to do with it, did it?"

She jerked away with such force that he found himself releasing her. Her back was to him, her head bowed, her hair streaming golden down her back in the moonlight.

"It really is late," she told him.

He bowed, indicating the stairs. "Please, you first."

He couldn't keep the bitterness out of his voice. She swung around, her head high again. "You aren't planning on throwing me down the ladder?" she inquired coolly.

"No. When I find some, I'll just throw you to the sharks. Though I doubt if they'll bite. Like recognizes like, you know."

"Really? Well, here's hoping *you* do fall to them, Captain Trellyn. Sharks can get into a frenzy and feed on each other. I'm sure you know how that works."

He stared at her, suddenly sorry. What should he do? Should he tell her he was so furious about Longford that he couldn't begin to be civil?

No, he didn't dare reveal that kind of emotion to Melinda.

He lifted his hands. "You're right. It's late. How about a truce for what remains of the night?"

She looked at him suspiciously.

He sighed. "I'm serious. I apologize. I'm not tossing you down any ladder, or to any sharks. They might come down with massive indigestion. No, no, just teasing, honest! I wouldn't want to let you go back to your father or Longford in anything less than the absolutely perfect shape in which you arrived."

"Roc Trellyn, if you—"

"Down, Melinda. I'm trying to stop. I'm tired. I wasn't expecting you, so you can't expect my manners to be great. Let's get some rest. Maybe things will improve tomorrow."

She stared at him for a moment, then turned and silently started down the ladder. He followed her.

She headed away from the galley and toward the captain's cabin.

He was right behind her.

She entered his cabin and started to shut the door quickly, but he caught it.

She stared at him. "You did tell me I was supposed to stay in here," she said.

"That's right." He forced the door open and followed her in, then closed it. She backed away from him, right into his desk, her eyes narrowed.

"If you think you can just—"

"Melinda, go to bed."

"You must be joking!"

"About what?" He sat in the chair, hiking his feet up on the desk, folding his hands in his lap and staring at her curiously.

"You're sleeping there?"

"Right here," he said lightly.

She bit her lip, lashes sweeping over her eyes for a minute.

Then she swung around and approached the bunk. It was broad, very comfortable. No room for complaint.

She stretched out, fully dressed, and turned her back on him. Then she swung around and stared at him again within a matter of seconds.

"This won't work."

"I'm very comfortable." He congratulated himself on being one hell of a liar.

"It's a big boat!" she told him.

"I've promised my crew that I'll be responsible for you and your whereabouts."

"Where can I possibly go—"

"Back down below. To the sonar, to our maps and plans."

"I was just—"

"Looking for the radio. I still want to know where you are."

"If I were to move—"

"From right here, I'd catch you!" he said softly.

"But I'm not—"

"Good. Then we can both get some rest."

She expelled another sigh of exasperation, staring at him hard.

"Good night, Melinda."

She swung around once again, her back to him. "This will not work!" she insisted again.

She sounded almost as desperate as he felt.

He leaned his head back. The chair was hard. Uncomfortable. He stared at the bed. Her hair was dry, falling all around her in golden waves. She was curved, tempting, soft, provocative....

He sighed.

She was right. It wasn't going to work. And now...

He clamped down hard on his teeth, swallowing a groan. Damn it!

He was going to sleep!

Despite the fact that the elegant beauty who slept just an arm's reach away in his bed was still his wife...

And despite the fact that he loved her still.

Chapter 4

He must have slept at some point during the night, because how else could he have woken up in such terrible pain? His neck hurt, his back hurt—hell, his whole damned body hurt.

And there she was. Sleeping just as sweetly as could be, all sprawled out, a vision in white and gold, arms embracing both his pillows, body cushioned by his mattress, one he'd ordered special, since he spent so much time on the boat.

Swearing softly, he rose, then banged his knee on the desk and swore again. Finally he stared at her.

She was still asleep. She didn't move a hair.

He couldn't take it. Muttering beneath his breath, he stumbled out on deck, where he ran right into

Connie, who was heading into the galley in her bathing suit and white robe.

"Good morning!" she said cheerfully, then backed away. "All right, so it's not such a great morning. But I've got the coffee on already. Maybe that will help. Then again, maybe not."

"Coffee sounds great," he muttered, walking past her to the port side of the boat.

"Where are you going?" she called after him.

"For a swim!"

"Now? The sun's barely broken. It will be cold."

"Good!"

He took a swift running leap up to the rail and plunged over.

Salty water greeted him. Nice and cold this early in the morning, even here in the Florida Straits. He plunged downward and downward with his dive, not fighting the momentum. A few seconds later he gave the water a firm shove and broke the surface once again. He swam hard toward the ship, feeling the familiar movements remove some of the aches in his muscles.

It was all her fault. Life had been going all right. At least he'd been sleeping.

Now she was sleeping beautifully while he had suffered the tortures of the damned all night. He didn't feel as if he'd slept a wink. He felt as if he could bite.

He would damned well like to run into his cabin, pick up his sweetly sleeping little beauty and throw her overboard into a nice, crisp awakening!

He reached the aft ladder, twelve feet from the rear of his cabin, and found that Connie was there to greet him once again, this time with a cup of steaming black coffee in her hands.

He accepted it gratefully and leaned on the rail, dripping beside her.

"Well," she said softly, "we thought that maybe you'd gotten lucky last night." She caught his glance and amended her words quickly. "Well, I mean, we thought that maybe there'd been some kind of a reconciliation. But the way that you woke up..." Her voice trailed away, and she looked out over the sea. "It's going to be a great day. A beautiful day for diving."

He grunted his agreement, staring out toward the horizon. For those who had actually slept through the night, it probably was going to be a beautiful day.

Connie started to say something else, but he raised a hand to silence her, then pressed his temple with his thumb and forefinger.

"Did you drink too much?" Connie asked solicitously.

"No, I didn't drink enough," he replied softly. He slid off the railing, slipping a hand around her shoulders. "Did you say breakfast is on? Maybe we should head into the galley while it's still edible."

"Edible! Oh, the bacon!"

Connie went racing ahead; he followed more slowly. Maybe breakfast would improve the morning.

Then again, maybe the morning was just doomed.

* * *

He seemed to be looking her way.

Melinda instantly dropped the curtain over the porthole again, sitting back on the bed, her heart beating too quickly, then seeming to become very heavy and fall into the pit of her stomach.

They'd looked so close, the two of them, so natural together. Connie handing him coffee, his fingers brushing hers as he took the cup. Then the soft conversation between them, their heads bent, nearly touching.

Melinda inhaled deeply and fought the sudden threat of tears. Well, what had she expected after three years? She'd had him once. And she'd lost him.

She lay back on the bed, still feeling an overwhelming sense of loss. She closed her eyes and wished that it weren't quite so easy to remember the past.

She would never forget the very first time she had seen him, standing beside her father. So tall, so dark, built like steel. She'd never seen a more arresting man, nor had she ever met one who seemed to make her feel quite so young or insecure. Her father seemed to live by his word—Roc Trellyn had been all that Jonathan had talked about since she had come to live with him. But she hadn't wanted to hear about anyone else, not then. She had been too wrapped up in herself, in her own guilt. She hadn't caused the accident....

But she hadn't been home when it happened, and that had added to the guilt. If she hadn't been out, she might have stopped her mother. At least that time. If she had just done something, she might have changed things. She couldn't manage to put her feelings of absolute failure into words, but of all people, her father should have been the one to understand how it was possible to love her mother for being sweet and beautiful and witty—and hate her at the same time. Sharon Davenport had died two days before her thirty-ninth birthday.

Melinda hadn't been able to talk to anyone, but at least, in her father's company, there was someone who had known Sharon, known her well, loved her. Jonathan was someone who could understand, someone she had needed badly at the time. He was removed, of course. He'd been gone for seven years. But he had still cared. He'd still felt the pain.

Melinda had been jealous of Roc Trellyn from the very first time she saw him.

And she had also been absolutely fascinated.

He was older than the college boys she had been dating, seven years older than she was. He was striking, and so assured, mature, his voice deep and strong, his eyes touched with wisdom. He was so handsome, broad at the shoulders, muscled in the right places, slim in others. She wanted to keep her father away from him, but she wanted to be near him herself.

Somewhere along the line, she realized that she simply wanted him. And then the fear of wanting someone so much—especially Roc Trellyn, who seemed to have someone waiting at every port—added to her discomfort. She didn't keep her distance any longer; she seemed intent on picking fights, on making sure that he saw that though others might faint at his feet, she couldn't care less.

But then there had come that day when they had been inadvertently thrown together in the same room, when she had felt his eyes on her, felt the length of her body burn from head to toe. She hadn't known what she intended at first—only to apologize. She had been rotten, she had tried to irritate him, and she had also tried to make sure she didn't pull any of her little tricks in front of her father. Maybe she couldn't have him, but at least they could be friends.

But then he had talked to her, as even her father hadn't talked to her, and it felt as if the weight of the world had been lifted from her shoulders. She could remember staring into the depths of his blue eyes, seeing the passion in them, hearing him reassure her.

Then she could remember wanting him once again. And, at long last, having him . . .

She trembled suddenly and leaped up from the bed. She strode quickly to the not-so-small head in the Captain's cabin and stood beneath the shower, anxious for the water to wash over her.

There had been no one in the world like Roc. No one to hold her, reassure her, love her. No one with his gently spoken wisdom.

And then again, no one with his shouted commands when he was on to something!

No one more stubborn.

No one fairer to a crew, more willing to listen.

Stop! she warned herself. She didn't dare fall headlong into the trap of wanting him again, of loving him....

Then just why was she here? she challenged herself.

To make sure that the big claim was his this time, that he found his *Contessa,* that she helped to make sure he wasn't cheated a second time....

Because she knew now that her father had been wrong, that Roc's accusations had been hard, but that he had been right to walk away. She hadn't known it then, though; she hadn't seen it. Her father had given Roc his start, trained him like a son. She had only seen Roc turning his back on her father after all that. It had never occurred to her that Jonathan might be wrong, that Roc's words might be true. She simply hadn't been capable of believing any ill of her father. So now...now she had to make sure things did go his way. He had always said everyone else was wrong about the *Contessa.* And he had been right. Now the world would soon be congregating in this vicinity, seeking the lost ship. But by all rights she should be Roc's. Melinda was a good diver, and she really could help.

And was that all she wanted? To fix things? she taunted herself.

No...

She had always wanted Roc. And she still did.

But it was too late. She had known it when she watched him sitting on the rail, his fingers curled around the cup of coffee another woman had given him. Their heads had been bowed, close together. He had laughed softly, touching Connie's shoulder with obvious affection.

Well, what had she expected? It had been a long time. Three years since he had left.

She'd never, ever realized he really meant to go. He'd held her so tenderly that night, made love to her so passionately. And then he had been gone....

And she hadn't been able to believe the ache, the void, the pain.

Only pride had kept her from going after him, that and the fear that he wouldn't want her again once he had left her behind.

The water was still running. She turned it off quickly, stepped out of the shower stall and shivered. Three years, and here she was, in his cabin, a most unwelcome guest—or a prisoner. It all depended on which way one chose to look at it.

And once again he'd managed to walk away. The thought brought tears to her eyes, and she quickly blinked them away.

Well, she wasn't staying in this cabin any longer, not unless he wanted to slide a bolt across the door.

And she could smell the tempting aroma of bacon. It made her stomach somersault as she realized just how long it had been since she had eaten.

She quickly donned her borrowed clothing again, then found his brush on the back of the sink and borrowed that. When she was done, she rummaged until she found an extra toothbrush in a case, and then she stared at herself in the mirror. Her eyes were too wide, too lost, too frightened. She lifted her chin. Better, a little better.

Then she took a deep breath and turned, determined. It was time to face the sea beasts!

Breakfast was on the table, a huge plate of bacon and sausage, muffins, toast and rolls, eggs scrambled with peppers and tomatoes. Despite the food, Roc had his maps out, ten of them in a bound roll. With his finger he traced a course from their position in the Florida Straits past Andros in the Bahamas and onward to a few of the smaller islands. "Now watch," he murmured, flicking the first map over and showing the group a more detailed map of the area, one that identified all the smaller islands, inhabited and not, and the reefs around them, with emphasis on the ones that jutted into the water with little warning, causing danger to ships. "She's here, right around this reef, and as soon as we've cleaned up, that's where I want to head. Joe—" he began, then broke off.

Silently, lithely, she had come into the galley. Bathed, freshened, smelling as sweet as a field of roses, her beautiful face scrubbed clean, her golden hair a mane around her shoulders, Melinda had made her way to them at last.

She ignored him at first, greeting Connie with a cheerful, "Good morning!" Then she looked around at the rest of the crew, her smile in place. She extended a hand to Bruce. "Well, I suppose you all know who I am, and in a rather strange way we've already met, but I'd like to make a few amends and do it a little bit better, if you all don't mind. I'm Melinda Davenport—"

"Trellyn, isn't it?" Connie asked softly.

Melinda flushed a lovely shade of rose. It only added to her charm, Roc decided. "I'm not really sure," she murmured, and hurried on, flashing Connie another smile and starting with Bruce.

"You're Connie's brother, Bruce. She told me that last night, while I was borrowing her clothes. And you...?" she inquired politely, facing Marina and Joe.

She had such a sweet smile on her face. They must all be thinking that he was either a complete bastard or a huge fool not to have managed to get along with her. In fact, they all looked a little hypnotized.

It was time to cut in.

"Joe Tobago and his wife, Marina. And Peter here rounds out my crew. Now if you're—"

"I'm starving," she said softly, smiling once again. "It smells absolutely delicious in here."

Marina nodded, and Bruce suddenly leaped up. "Sit down. I'll get you coffee."

"How nice, thank you, but I can see the pot on the stove. I'll get it myself."

She did so, walking toward the stove, finding a cup, helping herself. She came back to the table and looked down at the map. Roc clenched his teeth and carefully rolled up the lot of them.

"Excuse me," she said softly. "Deep dark secrets."

"You're a spy," he reminded her politely.

"A prisoner now," she said lightly. "Aren't prisoners supposed to be fed?"

"Bread and water," he said flatly.

"Please, sit!" Marina said, casting Roc a stern gaze. "You must be starving. You ate nothing last night. The plates are there, help yourself."

"Thank you," Melinda said, and did so. Roc leaned back. She was comfortable. Just as comfortable as she had been last night, while he had suffered the tortures of the damned in a hard chair. "I do apologize if I was rude to you yesterday," she told Bruce.

"Oh, it's all right, really. You *were* in a net—"

"Enough!" Roc said irritably. "She was caught in a net because she meant to be there. Marina, is there any more coffee over there?"

"Aye, captain!" Marina murmured, going for the coffeepot. Roc stared hard at Melinda, who stared back innocently.

"You look extremely well-rested," he commented.

"It's a very comfortable cabin."

"Bathed and fresh."

"The water pressure in your shower is magnificent," she replied politely. "And I took the liberty of borrowing a toothbrush from the pack of extras under the sink. There were a number of them."

Um. He wasn't the one who kept all the extra toothbrushes aboard, Marina was. But they were kept under the sink in his cabin simply because he had the most room. But he knew that Melinda must be wondering just how often he entertained in his cabin to keep such a collection of extra toothbrushes.

Good. Let her wonder. He had his own tortured thoughts to live with.

Longford!

Damn! He wanted to gag each time he thought the name. Wanted to pick her up and shake her...

He stood quickly, nearly knocking into Marina and the coffeepot she had just brought so she could pour him more coffee. "Bruce, we need to get under way. Let's pull anchor and start moving."

"Aye, captain!" Bruce agreed.

He paused to let Marina finish filling his cup, and by then Melinda was ready with one of her innocent questions. "So you're diving today? Where are we heading?" Aquamarine eyes, wide, innocent, looked around the cabin.

They'd all nearly dropped their tongues on the floor over her—Bruce, Peter, even Joe. And somehow she seemed to be gaining the sympathy of the women in the crowd. Roc waited for one of them to tell her exactly where they were going to look for the *Contessa*.

But they all seemed to have retained some sense of loyalty. There was silence in the cabin.

He smiled, leaning toward her. "You're not supposed to tell spies what you're up to and where you're going, Ms. Davenport."

Bruce nudged him. "Trellyn," he whispered. "She's still a Trellyn, isn't she?"

Roc raised himself up, meeting her eyes. "I'm not so sure she ever was!" he exclaimed softly; then, despite the liquid beauty of Melinda's eyes, so determined upon his, he swung around to leave the cabin.

She jumped up, following him. "Roc!"

He paused at the steps leading to the upper deck, looking back. They still had an audience.

"What?" he asked impatiently.

"Let me dive."

"You must be insane."

She threw up her arms. "What am I going to do?" she inquired almost desperately. "I'm a prisoner here. Where can I go with any information? Who can I tell?"

"There's still a radio on this boat!" he reminded her.

"And you won't let me use it."

"I won't always be aboard—"

"But your crew—"

"Don't know you—and your loyalty to your father—quite the way I do, Melinda!" he reminded her softly. So softly that their audience couldn't hear him.

It was almost amusing. The whole group of them suddenly seemed to lean forward en masse, trying to catch his words.

"I told you, my father—"

"Right. Longford let you out in the middle of the ocean. That's even worse."

He spun around, determined not to be stopped.

"Roc—"

He swung to face her once again. "Go do the dishes!" he snapped irritably.

She stared at him, her fingers clenching into fists at her sides, her chin still high, her eyes more dazzling, but damp, as if she might really care.

He'd seen those eyes look like that before. . . .

She turned around, and he did likewise, a little blindly, hurrying up the steps to the deck. He headed for the anchor winch and automatically set it in motion, rolling up the heavy anchor from the bottom of the sea. Bruce was quickly there beside him. "Take her up!" Roc said, leaving him to finish the task while he climbed to the elevated helm to stare out at the horizon.

He'd been careful in the last week. He knew right where he wanted to search, but he didn't want to anchor too near the spot by night, and he had changed his anchorage every night so as not to arouse suspicion in those who might be watching him.

Obviously he had been found anyway. Melinda was aboard.

But he hadn't been discoverd actually diving, and that, at least, was good.

Bruce called to him that the anchor was up, and he flipped on the switches for the motor, idled a moment, then took the big wooden wheel and started a course toward the Bahamas, toward a deserted island near the southwest section of the Northwest Providence Channel and a treacherous reef that had once caused danger to the great ships seeking the riches of the New World.

The *Crystal Lee* was a smooth-running, fast boat, and he quickly felt the cool rush of the morning air touching his face, sweeping back his hair. The sun was rising now; it was going to be a hot day, just barely cooled by the sea breezes.

It felt good to stand against the soothing, salt-laden wind. It helped to clear his mind after his difficult night, and it seemed he reached his destination far too soon.

He cut the motor and called down to Bruce to cast the anchor. They were off the reef by a good fifty feet, but the water here was still no more than fifty or sixty feet deep. He hurried down from the helm, only to discover that Melinda was there with the others, dressed once again in her black bathing suit, waiting patiently.

"Bruce, you've checked the tanks?" he asked his friend, staring at Melinda all the while.

"Joe and I did. Checked and rechecked."

His equipment was on the deck. Joe Tobago, who would be staying aboard, reached for Roc's tanks and mask and helped him into them. Connie and Bruce had helped each other, and there was Melinda, giving a hand to Peter.

Roc thanked Joe briefly and accepted his flippers, then found that Melinda was staring at him. "You're not diving," he said curtly.

"But—"

"Go—"

"Don't tell me to go do the damned dishes! I already did them. You can ask Marina!" she informed him in a vehement rush.

"You're still not diving!"

"You can't keep me out of the water!" she cried.

He looked over at Joe. "If you see another boat, any boat, near us, lock her up somewhere. It could be Longford trying to pull her back out of the sea."

"Roc, you have no right—"

"I have every right!"

He didn't wait for her reply but sat on the edge of the boat, then rolled backward into the water, setting his mouthpiece into place. Seconds later he was alone, accompanied only by the lulling sound of his regulator as he breathed in and out, sinking lower and lower into the sea. The blue and green seemed to close around him, and the cool, floating feeling that he loved so much entered into him, easing tension swiftly from his limbs. God, it was wonderful. It was another world, where all the rules changed and a man became nearly weightless, where the sweet sound of silence blanketed the harshness of the world above the surface.

He was nearing the reef, with the highest point jagging up to about fifteen feet below sea level, when he heard a sudden whooshing sound.

Another body in motion in the water near him . . .

Like a small dolphin.

Or a five-foot-eight-inch woman.

He turned his head. There she was. No tanks—neither Joe nor Marina would have betrayed him so far—no mask, no flippers. Just Melinda, with her incredible swimming skills and her near record-breaking ability to hold her breath.

She was swimming below him, golden hair following in her wake. She was as graceful, as fluid as any fish or creature of the sea, and truly, at that moment, she might have been a mermaid, a siren, one of Neptune's daughters, reigning supreme in the beautiful blue-green waters.

Damn her hide!

He plunged downward, swimming after her. She had gone past the reef, over to the other side, where the World War Two shipwreck lay strewn about.

Even as he pursued her, she disappeared inside the hulk.

"Melinda!" He started to scream her name, nearly choked, then swore at himself for being a fool.

Then he started after her in furious pursuit.

Chapter 5

He followed her across the rusting hull and in through a door that hung eerily on half of its hinges. The sunlight that had streaked through the beautiful blue-green water was dimmed within the confines of the rusted old hulk. Crossing a deck filled with cramped living quarters, he came to the point where damage and time had worn the downed ship completely in two. There was a near-barren expanse of sand, with just a few areas of haphazardly thrown seaweeds, coral and delicate, beautifully colored little sea creatures. The rest of the rotten ship had fallen over the shelf and lay another twenty feet deeper, about a hundred yards away.

Melinda was just disappearing over the ledge that led that twenty feet downward.

He caught her halfway down. She stared at him furiously, trying to shake free. How long had she been holding her breath now? It was uncanny.

He forced her to take his mouthpiece. She inhaled a vast supply of air, then tried to escape his hold once again, but he held onto her tightly. He pointed to the surface and let her know that he was taking her there—whether she wanted to go or not.

He gave a good kick, and they went shooting upward together. His legs brushed hers in the water, and he was startled by the erotic impact that slight touch seemed to have on him. She was sleek here under the sea. Tempting, even as he longed with all his heart to wring her neck.

They broke the surface, and he spat out his mouthpiece. "What do you think—"

"I'm not diving, I'm swimming!" she said irritably.

"What you're doing is dangerous, and you know it!"

She was silent for a moment, her lashes sweeping her cheeks. She knew it was dangerous to crawl around the old hulk the way she'd been doing. She could too easily become trapped by some falling piece of rot.

She opened her eyes again, staring straight at him. "Then what you're doing is dangerous, too!"

"But I have air tanks—"

"And you should still be with someone."

"Well, if I weren't following you around, I *would* be with someone!"

"If you don't let go of me, you're going to drown us both!"

"Ah!" he exclaimed, but his hold on her didn't ease in the least. "That's it. I've got it now. You're not a spy. You're just here to torment me to death so your father—or Longford—has time to move in for the find!"

"I'm not tormenting you—you're tormenting me. And if you'd just let me help you... I'm a damned good diver!"

"Out!" he told her, giving her a shove toward the ship.

"You don't rule the ocean!" she cried, treading water.

He lunged toward her. She started swimming again, at first slipping easily away, since she was unencumbered, but then the added power of Roc's flippers kicked in, and he overcame her about halfway between where they had been and the *Crystal Lee*.

"I said, out of the water!"

"And I said it's a free ocean!"

"Not while you're on my boat."

"I'm not on your boat, I'm in the water."

"If you don't quit arguing with me, I'll haul you out of the water and—"

"Oh, big talk! You wouldn't dare. Your crew would mutiny!"

"I dare just about anything, and you ought to know that by now, so there's just one question left—is that a challenge, Ms. Davenport?"

She jerked free of his hold, trying for a deep dive that would bring her back to the coral shelves, but he caught her first. With a firm hand on her arm, he started swimming hard for the *Crystal Lee.* She was strong, struggling and wriggling like a game fish on a line. But he reached the boat and the ladder, thrusting her toward it, then grabbing hold himself to force her ahead of him. Joe and Marina were on deck, anxiously waiting. Melinda leaped easily aboard, then disappeared into the captain's cabin with a quick nod to the others.

Roc struggled up more slowly, because of his gear. Fine, she was in his cabin. They would have a little privacy.

Right. With everyone on board listening just a few feet away!

"Eh, captain, I give you a hand!" Joe said, quickly coming over to take the tanks.

Roc ripped off his mask, breathing deeply, trying to control his temper. Even as he did so, Connie broke the surface, calling out, "We're coming up. It's a wash so far, Roc. We haven't found a thing."

He gritted his teeth. What was Melinda up to? He hadn't realized it, but an hour had gone by, and she had kept him occupied all that time.

Was that her job? To sabotage his search?

He started for the cabin, but Melinda suddenly burst out of it, a towel around her shoulders. Her eyes met his, and he almost smiled.

He knew her so well.

She'd run to the cabin first for protection. Then she'd realized that it was the one place where he could get her alone—and where she couldn't bat her lashes in hopes of help from the others.

He was still staring at her when Peter and Bruce crawled aboard, too, releasing their tanks, pulling off flippers and masks.

"Nothing," Bruce muttered disgustedly.

"Well, not nothing," Peter said with a shrug.

"We found some skulls," Connie informed him. She shuddered a little. "Eerie. I never came across part of anyone who'd ever been living before."

Bruce leaned against the wall of the elevated helm. "But not a darned thing on the *Contessa*."

"Actually," Melinda said softly, and suddenly all eyes were upon her, "I think I might have found something. Perhaps it did belong to the German ship, but it seems like it might come from before that. . . ."

Roc, no less amazed than everyone else, watched as she slipped a long sand-encrusted item from the side of her leg, held there by the elastic on her bathing suit.

He strode quickly across the deck. She held it out to him, one brow lifted in a definite challenge, her lip curled into a delicate smile.

"What is it?" Connie cried.

"Tableware of some kind," Melinda said, her eyes still on Roc. He hadn't taken the piece from her; he hadn't said a word.

She extended it to him. He wondered if it was like some kind of an olive branch.

For a long moment he didn't reach for it. Damn her. Down there with no tanks, with him following her, dragging her up.

And she was still the only one among them to come up with anything that might have even a remote possibility of coming from the *Contessa*.

"Roc?" She said his name softly, questioningly. He wasn't even sure the others could hear her.

He took it from her at last. It was heavily encrusted with sand and growth, but he had a hunch. She was right. He didn't think that a relic from the German boat would be so heavily encrusted. It was heavy in his hand, too—and not just from all the sand.

Just as he had always had a feeling about the *Contessa* being in this area, he now had a feeling that the object in his hand was from the lost ship.

"I'll take a look at it," he said, his eyes on hers. "Just where did you pick it up?"

She shrugged, then shook her head. "I'm not sure. I'd have to go back. I'd be more sure, of course, except that I wasn't paying attention at the time. I thought a shark or something was following me. Of course, when I turned back, I saw it was you, but I was nervous and, naturally, forgetful."

"Naturally!" he muttered, and spun away from her. Ignoring all of them, he hurried down the steps to the galley, then down the second flight to the equipment room below. He drew out a cloth and set the long object on it, then found a small mallet and painstakingly began to chip away at some of the growth.

It was a slow task. It required infinite patience. And he was good; he usually had all the patience he needed.

But he wasn't alone. One by one, they all followed him, Bruce and Connie, Peter, Marina and Joe and, *naturally,* Melinda.

There just wasn't enough room for the whole lot of them to sit there breathing at him.

With a sigh, he looked up. "Give me a little air, okay? I'll report the minute I know something."

Joe, always the wisest and most levelheaded of the group, nodded.

"Eh, 'e's right! 'E can't breathe down here. Wife, come on. Let's lie in the sun a while, eh?"

Marina quickly went up. Joe arched a dark brow at Connie. A little unhappily, she went. Then Peter, though not without saying, "Call me if you need me." Bruce shrugged and followed them.

Only Melinda remained.

He stared at her.

"Well, I did find it," she said softly.

"But you were on my expedition," he reminded her.

"Just as you were on my father's expedition—" she began.

"No! *Not* just as I was on his expedition, and if he ever chose to tell you the truth about it, you just might believe that. But it's too late, isn't it, Melinda? You simply chose not to believe in me—not to come with me. But I'll tell you what, if this proves to be a piece from the *Contessa,* I *will* do something for you that your father didn't do for me. I'll credit you for the dive!"

He was sorry for his outburst the moment it was finished. She stood very straight, without moving. She seemed to have gone pale beneath her tan, and her lashes had fallen over her marvelous aquamarine eyes. He saw the pulse beating at her throat. Indeed, he saw too much, because she was in that black bathing suit of hers that was not an erotic creation at all—except that it was on Melinda, and he could see the shapely, golden length of her legs and remember, could stare at the golden length of her neck and hunger. Could look at her lips and want to leap up, forget the past, forget the *Contessa,* forget even that there were five other people aboard the boat, and certainly forget himself...

"I don't need credit for the dive," she said with quiet dignity. "It's just that I did find the piece, and I'd like to see if it's worth anything or not."

He stared at the piece in his hand, then chipped at it again. His fingers were shaking.

He looked at her. "Melinda, give me a few minutes on my own. Let me get closer to the piece itself; then you can come back when we get to the cleaning."

She lowered her head again, then nodded and turned, and he found himself watching her every movement as she crawled up the ladder.

Back, buttocks, legs.

He tried to stare at the piece. His fingers were still shaking. His body felt as hot as molten lead, as tense as piano wire.

He sat back, seething, wanting to wring her neck again.

Wanting her.

He looked at the piece, trying to concentrate. He needed her off the boat. He closed his eyes for a minute, willing his hands to be still. He went back to his task, slowly, carefully, chipping away.

He hit the right place. Barnacles and grit broke away in his hands. He leaped up, going to a cabinet for cleaning solution, then dipping some onto a cloth and rubbing at the piece.

It began to gleam a beautiful silver. Carefully, he rubbed farther.

Finally he sat back, staring at it. Then he leaped up again, finding a magnifying glass, studying the piece with high excitement.

It was a spoon. Elaborate, definitely Spanish, definitely very, very old...

From the *Contessa*. It had to be.

He studied the design on the piece, then set it down very carefully. He picked up his copy of the ship's manifest and leafed through it quickly.

Eighty-eight silver spoons had been aboard, crested with a likeness of a crown.

He looked at Melinda's find again. Once more his fingers began to shake. They were close. So close. The *Contessa* was here—somewhere....

He stood quickly, carrying the spoon with him, climbing to the galley deck. He started to shout, then realized that they were all there, seated around the galley table, looking like a troop of puppies at the pound that hadn't been adopted. Connie and Melinda were sipping tea; Bruce and Peter had beers. Joe was just sitting there drumming his fingers on the table, and Marina was behind him, her arms around his neck.

"My lord, this looks like a wake!" he said.

They turned, leaped up as one.

He produced the spoon.

"I checked the manifest. Looks as if this is definitely the real McCoy."

Connie let out a wild shriek and kissed Bruce on the cheek, Marina threw her arms around Joe, and Peter rushed forward to pump Roc's hand.

Roc stared over Peter's shoulder at Melinda, who just stood there alone, very quietly, aquamarine eyes steady on his.

"So you've found her!" Peter said. "The *Contessa!* Just like you always knew you would."

"*We've* found her," Roc murmured. And he walked forward, placing the spoon on the table in front of Melinda, his eyes still hard on hers. "Actually, Melinda found her, so it seems. Congratulations, Ms. Davenport."

He left the spoon sitting there, then turned and walked out of the galley, heading up the steps, anxious to get on deck, to feel the breeze tear through his hair, cool his face.

He set his hands on the port side rail. He should be ecstatic. Not that one spoon was proof positive of anything, but since he had always thought the *Contessa* was somewhere near here, it did seem like an awfully good indication that they had almost found the whole treasure.

So why didn't he feel ecstatic? His fingers curled tightly around the rail until the veins in his hands stood out. He looked down at them and released the rail quickly.

Maybe a shower.

He moved away from the rail and headed into his cabin. He kept the water chilly, then hot. He scrubbed his face, his hair, and reminded himself that when he reached land he really did need a haircut. The steam rose around him. He was using way too much hot water. At the moment, though, it felt good. It was easing the tension from his muscles.

He started, hearing, just above the rushing water, his cabin door opening. Hands that had been sluicing soap over his shoulders suddenly went still.

"Who the hell is it?"

There was silence for a moment.

"Who the hell—"

"It's me!" Melinda announced. "Damn, you're the one who insisted that this place be my particular prison."

"What?"

He'd heard her. At the moment, though, her words didn't make any sense.

She came closer. Looking over the glass enclosure of the small shower stall, he saw that she had come unhappily to the doorway.

"I said that you were the one to insist that your cabin was my prison! I'm sorry! I didn't mean to interrupt you. I was just going to take a shower. I didn't realize that you were already there, captain!" She offered him a quick salute, looking as if she were quite ready to flee, and not nearly so confident as she tried to sound.

But Melinda was always confident....

"I'll be out in a minute."

Suddenly the door to his cabin burst open, and Connie came rushing on in. "A picnic, that's it! A barbecue! We need to celebrate, and Teardrop Isle isn't a twenty-minute ride away. What do you think—oh!"

Bless Connie. When she was excited, she didn't see a thing, not a single thing even if it was right in front of her face. It had taken her that whole long speech to realize that Roc was in the shower and Melinda was standing in the doorway.

"Oh. Oh, I am sorry! I didn't realize. Forgive me, I—"

"Connie, damn it, there's nothing to forgive you for!" Roc grated in exasperation.

"I didn't mean to make you mad—" she began again, looking from Roc to Melinda, then back again.

"I'm not mad!"

"Then why are you shouting?" Connie demanded.

"You *are* shouting," Melinda told him with a shrug.

He placed his hands over his face and groaned softly. "Get out of here, both of you, please. Connie, I'm not mad, and a picnic sounds just like a little hunk of heaven. Melinda, the shower and the cabin will be all yours in just ten minutes. Now—out!"

Connie turned and fled instantly. Melinda stood there staring at him, aquamarine eyes glittering with anger.

"You just scared that poor girl half to death."

"She's not scared. She knows me too well for that."

"Really?"

Was there perhaps a touch of jealousy in the inquiry? Hard to tell. She had that regal look about her, chin high, eyes flaming, hair a fantastic golden mane. She leaned against the door frame, arms crossed over her chest, totally defiant. Well, why shouldn't she be? He never had seemed to carry out a threat with her. Except once.

He inhaled slowly, deeply. "She knows me well enough to get the hell out when I ask her to!" he snapped.

"Ah, yes, the great captain speaks! Let's all jump quickly or else walk the plank!"

"Out," he warned her.

She arched a brow.

The water seemed to have grown hotter and hotter. "If you're not out of here in thirty seconds, you'll be joining me for a shower," he warned.

"I'm simply trying to make the point that you can't yell at people and scare them just because *you're* in a foul mood because *I* found the proof *you* were looking for."

"Ten seconds."

"Roc, I told you—"

He pushed open the clouded shower stall door, and her eyes widened considerably. She stared at him quickly, hastily, from head to toe.

"Wait a minute—" she began.

"Time's up," he promised.

Well, she had surely seen him. All of him. Maybe it had even stirred a few memories.

What those memories were, he couldn't be sure, because she had turned to flee.

Too late. He had warned her.

His hands landed on her shoulders, and he spun her around, bending and throwing her over his shoulder.

A shriek left her, faint because he had left her so little breath with which to protest.

She was light, he thought. Despite her shapely, muscular strength, despite her five feet eight inches, she was light when he lifted her.

Skeins of soft golden hair tumbled over his naked back and shoulders. Teased his buttocks and beyond. Her fingers gripped his bare flesh as she struggled to escape.

He almost groaned aloud, it ached so to touch her, aroused things already aroused, things she surely had already seen, and yet, to his amazement, things that could feel an even greater call to hunger.

Touching her...

It was a mistake!

He walked quickly, intently to the shower stall and set her on her feet under the still rushing water. The water poured over her golden hair, soaking it, plastering it around her face. She stood beneath the heavy spray, gasping, steadying herself with her hands on his shoulders.

She looked into his eyes, her own burning. "You son of a—"

"You said you wanted a shower!" he reminded her, catching her hands, taking them from his shoulders. "Enjoy!"

He turned swiftly, closing the shower door behind him. Still dripping, he grabbed a towel and stepped into the cabin, swallowing hard, trying not to shout out loud. He dried himself in a fury, stepped into briefs and shorts, muttering beneath his breath all the while, furious with her, furious with what she could do to him.

He stared at the bathroom door. He was dressed now. Sort of. Halfway composed. And fair was fair.

He strode across the room, throwing the door open. As he had suspected, she had apparently been certain that he was gone.

She had stripped off the black suit with its sexy, nonexistent back and French-cut thighs. It was flung over the door of the stall.

She was facing the flow of water, scrubbing her face.

The misted panel of the shower door did little but add a fascinating intrigue to the shapely structure of her body. Naked, she seemed a work of art, her back so long, so beautifully curved, her hips flaring, her derriere rounded and perfect, legs so willowy and long. . . .

She swung around, her eyes meeting his and widening. "What—" she began.

"Thought you might be needing a towel!" he called out in a light tone, tossing his own on the hook. "Go right ahead. I didn't mean to interrupt you!"

His hand on the doorknob, he started to walk out, then paused for a second. "Gaining a few pounds, eh?"

It was a lie. She hadn't gained an ounce.

"What?" she demanded.

"Nothing."

"Will you get out?" she demanded.

He grinned. "Yeah, sure."

She spun around, reaching for the faucet, shutting the water off instantly.

He was going to leave. He was really going to leave. He meant to leave.

It was just that his feet wouldn't obey his mind's command.

He strode toward the stall instead, throwing the clouded glass door open once again.

And he reached for her, hands circling her waist, drawing her against his naked chest. He felt the thunder in her heart.

Felt the fullness of her breasts, the torment of her nipples grazing across his flesh, felt himself fitting against her despite the cutoffs he had donned.

She felt it, too. Everything. The stroke of flesh, the hardness of muscle—and of... other things.

Those beautiful eyes filled with alarm. Her voice was meant to be tough, filled with bravado. But her words faltered. "What the hell are you doing, Roc?"

What the hell *was* he doing?

"I forgot to thank you for sharing the spoon," he said softly, and before she could protest again, before she could move, he held her even tighter.

He'd been aching to do this. Dying to. He caught her chin with his free hand, lifting her face to his. Touched her lips with his own, covered them, engulfed them. Softly at first. Then with force, demandingly.

A protest sounded in her throat as his tongue parted her lips, her teeth. She squirmed in his hold, the movement of her breasts across his chest delicious.

His tongue slipped deeper into her mouth. Tasted, explored, played.

Her fingers froze on his upper arms. She was still, crushed against him, her heart hammering, slamming....

What in hell are you doing?

The question rose with cruel torment in his own mind. He had wanted to touch her; he had done so. And awakened all the fires of hell inside himself.

Damn...

He broke the kiss, met her blazing eyes. "Thanks," he forced himself to say softly. "Thanks very much."

"Damn you, Roc Trellyn!" she cried. "Get out!"

"Ms. Davenport, I am gone!" he promised.

Then, blindly, he managed to step from the shower stall.

And this time he left not just the shower but his cabin, swearing violently to himself that in the future he would remember to lock the damned door.

Chapter 6

Long after Roc had left the cabin, Melinda remained in the shower stall, shivering. Damn him. She had known what it would be like if he touched her again. She kept trying to tell herself that she was here because she owed him, but she was really here because she wanted him. But wanting was so foolish, so wasteful . . . so painful.

She should have kept her distance; she needed to be careful. She couldn't run around throwing out brash challenges, because . . .

Because she was the one who was going to get hurt. All over again.

At last she managed to reach for the towel he had tossed her way. His towel, she thought, roughly rubbing herself dry with it. Something of him seemed to linger about it, his clean scent, his . . .

She threw the towel aside, then realized she had nothing to wear except for the black bathing suit she had just discarded, the only piece of clothing aboard the boat she could call her own, or the white outfit she'd borrowed from Connie, but it was already feeling awfully grungy.

Well, she could always find something of his. After all, she had to have something to wear.

She bit her lip, feeling the shakes start again as she thought of the way he had kissed her. It had been more than a kiss. Roc could always make it more than a kiss. Somehow he kissed with all his body, and she felt all of his body with all of hers, and . . .

She could remember so clearly the feel of him. The hardness, the hunger, the sweet fire that seemed to sweep from him to her no matter how she tried to fight it.

And yet he had managed to set her aside and walk away. Just as he had done three years ago.

And here she was, back again.

Because I was wrong! she cried in silent anguish to herself.

It would serve him right, she thought, if she just waltzed out on deck stark naked and apologized for being a prisoner without any clean clothing. He was hardly sparing much thought to such matters. She would have been in dire trouble already, if it weren't for Connie.

Connie, who was so sweet, so nice. And who made Melinda so jealous.

She squared her shoulders and swallowed hard. Now, as to the matter of clothing...

She sighed deeply, fully aware that she wasn't going to prance anywhere naked.

Yet even as she stood there, wrestling with the dilemma, the pretty blonde with the enormous brown eyes tapped on the door to the cabin and stuck her head in. Melinda snatched the cast-aside towel from the floor and smiled wanly at the other woman.

"Thanks for coming. I was just looking at my limited wardrobe, and I think I definitely give new meaning to the words, 'I don't have a thing to wear.'"

Connie smiled. "I rather thought that. It's lucky we're about the same size, although, of course, you're taller. Actually," she mused, stepping back, "you're a lot more something-er in a number of ways."

Melinda raised an eyebrow. *"What?"*

"You've—you've just got a lot more shape."

Melinda was startled by the strange compliment. "Connie, trust me," she murmured in turn, "you're not lacking a thing. You're a beautiful woman, and you must know that."

Connie seemed equally startled. "Really?" she murmured.

Melinda frowned, amazed. "Really. Don't these goons around here let you know it now and then?"

"Well, Bruce is my brother, Joe is married, Peter is busy all the time, and..."

"And Roc?" Melinda asked softly.

Connie's lashes lowered. "Roc is a courteous man," she replied. "A busy one, too. And the boss."

And anything more? Melinda longed to ask, but she refrained. Roc was usually courteous. And he could be very kind. She should know that better than anyone else alive. He had dealt with her so gently—even when she had been entirely rotten to him—once she had admitted that she was hurt, lost and in pain.

And then I managed to lose him, she reminded herself.

She lowered her lashes quickly, gritting her teeth for a moment. She was going to get a grip on this thing. She should never have come out here.

And she would be an absolute idiot to let him get close to her. In his eyes she had betrayed him. He would never forgive her. And if he did touch her, it would be only to taunt her, as he had today.

He had proven how easily he could walk away. Twice now. No matter what she felt for him, she wasn't going to let him get close again.

She still loved him, but she couldn't afford to be used by him. And, God help her, maybe she was better off with him thinking she had come to spy. If he mistrusted her, held her an arm's distance away all the time, it would be much better.

Maybe I shouldn't have picked up the damned spoon, she thought. It had angered him somehow. He didn't believe she meant for him—*wanted* him—to make his claim.

Maybe that was good, too.

Roc had been right about the *Contessa* all along. She could remember sitting with him one night when they had taken one of her father's boats out alone for a weekend, just to be together.

She'd made dinner, the moon had risen, and she'd come out of the galley after cleaning up to find him with a book in his hands, a book on the *Contessa.* Somehow she had ended up curled in his lap, listening to him.

"They're all wrong, you know. Look at the course she took! She's here, right between the Florida coast of the old U. S. of A. and the Bahamas. She's right here under our noses!"

"Why hasn't she been found, then?" Melinda had asked, smiling, humoring him.

And he'd kissed her. "Because we sometimes lose sight of the treasures right beneath our noses!" he had assured her. And then they hadn't talked about it anymore, because he had kissed her, and they had stared up at the stars and the night, eventually becoming lost in each other. . . .

That was then, she reminded herself. And this was now.

And Connie was staring at her, reminding her that she had been in the middle of a conversation when she had lost herself in the past. Thinking back to that conversation she realized that Connie, almost unbelievably, didn't seem to be very confident about her beautiful blond appearance.

"Well," Melinda murmured, smiling at Connie again, "they're all goons if they don't take the time to notice now and again that you're a lovely woman. And I'm extremely grateful for the loan of clothing."

"It's hard to bring your own when you're planning on getting scooped up in a fishnet, huh?"

Melinda stared at Connie, wondering if there was rancor in the question. But she saw only amusement in the other woman's eyes, then found herself smiling in return.

"Right," she agreed.

Connie lifted her hands. She was carrying a bundle of clothing.

"More goodies. A few are from Marina—she has a few things I'm missing. Like boobs," she said a little mournfully, and Melinda laughed.

"Hey, yours are just fine. Remember that one day most of the world's big-breasted women will be sagging, but you'll keep a nice shape your whole life."

Connie laughed. "I'll try to look at it that way! Anyway, there's a whole lot of stuff here—bras, panties, shorts, shirts, a few beach cover-ups. Not more than a few days' worth, but we have a washer and dryer in the galley, and Marina says just throw your laundry to her whenever you want."

"Thanks," Melinda said softly.

When Connie threw the pile of stuff on Roc's bunk, Melinda studied her for a moment, her heart racing.

The woman just couldn't be having an affair with Roc. She wouldn't be so blasé about a suddenly returned ex-wife—who wasn't really *ex* at all—sleeping in Roc's cabin if there had really been anything between them.

"May I ask you a personal question?" Connie said, hesitating.

"Ask anything you like. Whether you'll get an answer or not..." Melinda said, and shrugged.

Connie grinned. "Are you spying? Did you know that this was Roc's boat? I mean, the dolphin thing—"

"I love dolphins!" Melinda promised vehemently. "And I *am* involved with a number of groups trying to educate fishermen in ways *not* to snare them and yet still manage to make their living from the sea."

Connie laughed. "Oh, I believe you love dolphins. I love them, too. So do most people. But, well, what were you *really* doing in our net?"

Melinda hesitated. "I had an idea that this boat wasn't a real fishing vessel. I thought that it might be searching for the *Contessa*."

"So you *were* spying!"

Melinda shook her head. "Not really. I want Roc to find this treasure. I don't know if you can believe me or not—I certainly don't expect you to—but I want this claim to be his. I'm not working for anyone."

"Not even your father?"

Melinda grinned. "You don't know my father, Connie. He doesn't need anyone spying for him. He'll do his own searching, in his own way. Except that I think—"

"Yes?"

Melinda shrugged again. "Actually, I think my father wants Roc to make this claim, too. Maybe we owe him. Both of us."

Connie watched her for a moment. "Actually," she said after a moment, "I *do* believe you." She turned, then paused at the cabin's doorway. "Hey, get dressed. We're taking the dinghy over to the island as soon as Roc brings the *Crystal Lee* a little bit closer in. It's a celebration!"

Connie left, closing the cabin door behind her. Melinda went to check out her new wardrobe, and chose a checked crop top and navy shorts. She felt the boat getting underway even as she buttoned her last button.

She turned to the dresser by the wall near the captain's bunk and found Roc's brush. She hesitated a minute, then began to stroke it through her drying hair. It took some time to work out the tangles. When she finished, she set the brush down and stared at her face, at her still too-wide eyes.

Don't look vulnerable! she warned herself. More than that, don't *be* vulnerable.

But she was.

They all seemed to think that she was protected by some kind of armor, that Davenport's daughter had to be as tough as nails. Well, good, let them think it. She did wear armor—her pride.

But there were chinks in that armor. Lots of them.

The boat had come to a stop again. She felt the rocking movement as it settled.

Roc shouted to someone to cast the anchor. Connie shouted to someone else to come help her with the bags.

Melinda set the brush down and hurried out, determined to help Connie.

After all, they were celebrating tonight.

It wasn't really night. It was the most beautiful time of day, the very beginning of sunset.

They brought the dinghy over to the uninhabited island just as the sun dipped to the water, throwing rays of gold and vibrant red across the blue of the sky and that of the sea.

Barefoot, like the rest of the group, Roc jumped into the water to drag the dinghy ashore. Peter leaped out swiftly after him, reaching in to grab a few of the bags Connie and Marina had packed. The rest followed quickly. Roc noticed that Melinda was fitting in annoyingly well, just as if she had been hired to hunt for treasure the same as they had been.

With the dinghy pulled up on shore and the others starting to dig a pit for the fire, he paused for a moment, staring from the beautiful sunset to the scene before him, Melinda down on her hands and knees alongside Marina, scooping up the sand and getting ready to lay the coals they'd brought.

The tension was getting to him again.

Her outfit didn't help.

She should be dressed in rags, ill-fitting things like potato sacks.

No, not even potato sacks could make her look unappealing.

But they wouldn't be as bad as what she had on. Short, *short* blue shorts, and a blue and white checked midriff thing that barely covered her. It hadn't been so long ago, of course, that he had seen her in nothing at all, so it was easy to imagine what lay beneath the wisps of clothing.

He gritted his teeth.

His ex-wife—all right, his *wife*—was definitely managing to create havoc in his life.

He kept staring at her, watching as Bruce said something, to which she smiled quickly in return.

The poor boy was going to trip over his own tongue if she kept smiling at him like that.

Roc started to walk a little way down the beach. When he stopped, he sat with his feet in the water, looking out on the horizon.

They'd spent so many nights like this, under red and gold sunsets, staring out at the endless sea.

Strange. Once he had known the lure of the sea was so totally in his blood, he'd never expected to meet anyone like Melinda. A woman who could live happily and easily aboard ship, swim like a fish—and look like an angel. He'd been sure he was meant to be a loner, but then he'd met Davenport's daughter. . . .

Not that things had been smooth. Melinda had always been determined, as he was reminded again and again now. They'd had a tendency to fight over the fact that she could be reckless—especially when she was determined. He'd hauled her out of the water a few times when she'd gone on some search alone, and they'd both yelled and argued, and he'd usually won, because he'd been right. But he'd also had his ways of making it up to her softly in the darkness, where the anger that had spurred him so hotly became a passion made all the sweeter by what had gone before.

And so things had gone—until the wreck of the *Infanta Beatriz.*

Like the *Contessa,* she had sailed for the New World from Spain. Legend had it that she sank off the northern tip of Cuba, and it was rumored that if she were found, she would yield little, because she had gone down in shallow waters and been stripped of her wealth long ago.

Still, Roc had read everything he could about her, fascinated by the promise of an unusual horde of jewels that might—or might not—have been aboard.

He had talked with Jonathan Davenport about the ship, had thrown all his enthusiasm into pleading that they hunt for her.

Davenport had been unconvinced, so Roc had spent his free time searching for her, out on his own.

The lure hadn't really been the value of the treasure, nor even the idea of showing off what he had steadfastly sought and discovered, despite the skepticism of others.

After all, in the end, he dived for the love of diving, not for gain. Like any hunter, his thrill was in the chase.

But he had by chance been with Davenport when he discovered a lady's chest from the ship, deeply encrusted, yet yielding a startling cache of perfect golden coins. He had barely managed to clean a few when he discovered that Davenport had called a press conference and laid claim to the *Infanta Beatriz*. And when Roc protested in anger, Davenport insisted that the search vessel had been his—damn the long days Roc had searched alone!—and that Roc was simply working for him. He had known, of course, that they were looking for the ship.

Despite the fact that he had refused to do so.

Roc could never forget the anger he'd felt. Or what had awaited him after he'd hurried to his cabin, assuming that Melinda would be equally outraged.

Oh, she had been outraged, all right. But not on his behalf. It *was* her father's ship, she insisted.

"How can you be so ungrateful? Everything you've done, you've done with my father!"

"Melinda, he didn't want to be bothered with the *Infanta*. He did everything he could to keep me from even looking for her!"

He could still remember her behavior that night. She had undoubtedly overheard the wild argument between her father and her husband, but she had simply showered, then sat before the small dressing table in a white terry robe and brushed her hair. She had barely turned when he had walked in, instead meeting his eyes in the mirror.

He should have known then. She might be his wife, but first and foremost she was Davenport's daughter.

"Roc, what difference does it make? His find, your find. There will be more ships—the sea is littered with them."

He had walked over to her then. "No more ships together," he said softly. "We're leaving in the morning."

She'd set the brush down at last. "Don't be ridiculous! Of course you'll find more ships together. My father's humored you all along, searching for the *Beatriz.* Roc, you have to give him his due. I think—"

"I think your father's mad that I was right, and he just can't admit it."

"And I think you're acting like a spoiled two-year-old. My father said he gave you his blessing, that he traveled where you suggested, that he put as much energy into the search as into any other. My father—"

"Your father is a liar and a cheat—"

Suddenly she was on her feet, her hand cracking across his chin. He couldn't remember having been more furious in all his life, but he managed just to catch her up, his fingers wound around her wrists, and tell her succinctly, "I'm leaving first thing in the morning. You have tonight to decide if you're my wife or his daughter."

She paled at that. Her head back, her eyes sizzling, she insisted, "You have no right to walk out! I *am* your wife—but I'm his daughter, too."

"We're leaving."

"We're not! You'll make up in the morning."

"No, Melinda, we will not. I'm leaving."

And he was. He knew it with complete certainty. Everything inside him ached as if a limb were being detached. Davenport had been his boss, his mentor, his best friend—and his father-in-law. But he couldn't accept what Davenport had done. He was too damn good at what he did to be ridiculed—and then used.

"Are you with me?"

She'd wrenched away from him, and he had known her answer. She wasn't with him but with her father.

The ache within him deepened. He had loved her. Really loved her. Loved her raw determination, her wild reckless spirit, the way she was so swift to teach others, to help them, to give to them. So aloof at times, so independent, and yet so quick to come to him, to curl against him and trust in him, to dream with him beneath a star-laden canopy over a gently rolling sea.

No more. Her trust was in her father.

So this was it. Their last night.

He was still seething with anger, besieged with pain. But she stood with her back to him, her shoulders square, as if determined to keep the argument going.

But he knew it was over. He walked across to her, lifted her hair, kissed her neck. She turned to argue; he slipped his hands beneath the neckline of the terry robe and sent it floating to the floor. She opened her mouth to speak, and he closed it for her with the seal of his own. For brief seconds she was rigid. . . . Then she returned his passion wildly, sweetly.

Perhaps she was trying to convince him to stay.

Just as he wanted her to ache in the night once he was gone.

He didn't sleep. He rose at dawn and packed his belongings, leaving most of his equipment. She was still asleep. He sat by the bed and woke her at last, feeling once again as if he were losing some piece of his body. Perhaps his heart.

Perhaps his soul.

She woke slowly, eyes so beautifully dazed, body sleek, hair tumbling all about her.

"Are you coming?" he asked simply.

"You can't just walk out on him!" she cried, aquamarine eyes suddenly wide and ablaze.

That was it. He turned and started out the door.

"Don't you ever, *ever* come back!" she cried fiercely.

He turned once. "If you decide to choose me over your father, you're welcome to come after me."

"You're really leaving? Just like that? After all that he's done? After last night?"

"Yes."

Her chin went up. "I hate you!" she whispered fiercely.

Her lower lip was quivering, the sheet falling from her shoulders. Her eyes were glittering. With fury? With tears?

He dropped his bag and found himself beside her again, taking her into his arms, unable to keep from touching her. Her fists slammed against his shoulders and his back; then her fingers began to dig into his flesh. "I hate you, I hate you, I hate you!" she cried. But she held him. Held him as he kissed her, touched and savored the length of her, tried to tell himself that there were other women in the world. He knew that he had come back this time because he couldn't bear to go, that he had to remember her, each curve of her, each taste of her. Yet, once again, the passion and the fury were finally spent. And she whispered softly, "I couldn't believe that you would really leave me."

"I'm not leaving you. I'm leaving your father."

She went still, then became a whirlwind of motion, sweeping the covers around her, drawing to the head of the bed, staring at him with eyes as hard as gemstones. "You mean that you—"

"Melinda, I've said it a dozen times now. I'm leaving! I'm leaving your father's employ, I am not leaving you. If you insist on staying, you are the one who is leaving me."

He turned his back on her; he had to. He dressed methodically, not turning around.

"I hate you!"

The words burned into his back.

"Melinda—"

"If you're going, go. Get out!"

He reached for her, but she jerked farther away, as if she could merge with the wall.

"Go!" she whispered.

It was the only thing left to do. He turned, and that time he left for real. But all the while he walked down the dock, he prayed that she would appear behind him, perhaps yelling, perhaps indignant, telling him again that he had no right, telling him anything, trying to convince him to stay.

But she didn't appear. Still, they were in Key West, and he made his every move for the next few days just as obvious as possible. Anyone could have found him—if they had wanted to.

Melinda hadn't wanted to.

I hate you, she had said. Words of passion, of anger, spoken in a rush. She couldn't have meant them.

But perhaps she had.

Because two days later her father's ship headed out to sea, and Melinda sailed with him.

He hadn't seen her since. He'd heard about her, of course. She'd made a few finds of her own over the last few years, and every time her father was mentioned, she was, too, of course. The press loved Davenport and his beautiful daughter. Everyone loved a mermaid.

He pulled himself to the present and discovered that the sun had nearly set.

They'd gotten a nice fire going on the beach, and its yellow flames were competing with the colors in the sky. Roc frowned suddenly, staring past the fire.

Joe had the grill set up over the coals in the sand pit, and Connie and Marina were busy setting fish fillets and chicken pieces atop it. Peter was stirring some concoction in a pan at the edge of the heat, and Bruce leaned back on a bunched-up towel, a beer in his hand, supervising the lot of them.

"Careful with the fish now, Marina. Those fresh fillets don't need more than five minutes a side!"

Marina's dark eyes rolled his way in warning.

Roc leaped to his feet, aware that Melinda was nowhere to be seen. He strode to the fire. "Where is she?" he asked, a scowl knitting his brow. He was amazed at the worry, the fear, the anguish, that had seized hold of him.

Bruce seemed startled by the tension in his voice. They all stared at him for a moment.

"She just went for a walk around the island," Bruce said. "There's nowhere for her to go from here, Roc. I mean, she can't possibly be reporting to anyone."

"No, the little fool could be in the water again!" he muttered darkly. "Which way did she head?"

Bruce pointed down the beach to his left.

"The waters are calm, not much current, and the cove on the other side is well protected," Marina reminded him quietly.

He nodded briefly, then turned and started down the beach.

His strides were long. There wasn't much daylight left. The red streaks were now being overtaken by the darkening grayness of the swiftly coming night.

They simply didn't know her. It was one of the things they had fought about the most. She always taught others never to siwm or dive alone, but she seemed to think herself invincible, and whenever she was upset, which undoubtedly she was right now, she always seemed to go straight for the water. There were so many dangers at night. On a dive in the daylight, they both knew how to deal with curious sharks. But at night, there could easily be some hungry predators ready to find her appetizing. Makos, lemon sharks, hammerheads, blues and more frequented these waters.

He lengthened his strides. His heart thundering, he passed a big clump of trees, but he didn't see her yet. He walked over a sand dune and into a cove protected on all sides by brush and hills of sand. It was getting so damn dark!

"Damn her!" he muttered, his fear increasing. He looked up at a sudden fall of light. The moon had been up, big and full already, even while the last vestiges of day remained. It had been hidden by a dark cloud, which now had drifted away.

He saw her at last.

She was there, just staring out to sea. Tall, slim, alone, her chin high, her shoulders straight, her back to him.

It was how she had looked that last night. So determined to stand against him.

And just as he had wanted to touch her that night, he wanted to touch her now.

No. Just as he had *wanted* her that night, he *wanted* her now.

Fool . . . to think he had left all that behind.

He found himself walking silently down to her, pausing for a moment just behind her as the breeze lifted her hair.

He stepped closer. Her shirt left her shoulders bare, and his left hand settled on her upper arm, while his right hand lifted the wealth of golden hair from her nape. He pressed his lips to the flesh he'd bared, breathing in the sweet scent of her.

She stiffened slightly. Shoulders so square, back so straight. She was probaby going to spin around and slap him any second. . . .

But she didn't. His kiss moved from her nape over her shoulder, the tip of his tongue searing her flesh.

He felt the hunger in him. Felt the slight trembling that had begun in her . . .

"Roc," she murmured softly, starting to shift.

"No," he murmured, not willing to listen to any protest. His fingers caught the elastic of her borrowed shirt, and he tugged it downward, baring her breasts. Arms laced around her from behind, he cupped her breasts with his hand, callused flesh rounding over her nipples. She moaned softly as he continued to caress her. Kiss her. Slowly, so slowly.

Savoring each sweet, erotic brush of his roughened hands over her silken skin.

He eased the shirt down farther. Over her midriff, still touching, still stroking. He found the waistband of her navy shorts, the button, the zipper. He opened both, his hand sliding down against her belly, then farther still, fingers brushing over the soft golden triangle there.

A strangled sound escaped her. He pressed closer against her back, his kiss finding her ear, her throat.

"Don't deny me!" he whispered harshly, feeling again the tempest of her trembling. Feeling the rise of his own hunger, the burning...

"The others—"

"They won't follow, I promise."

She was silent as he tugged on the shirt, her shorts, the panties beneath them. Slid them downward until they fell to the beach. She slipped her feet gracefully from the puddle of clothing, one at a time, then stood very still, the moonlight beaming down upon her shoulders.

At last she turned into his arms. Facing him. Naked once again.

"This is a mistake..." she began gravely, aquamarine eyes a tempest of confused longing.

"I've made lots of mistakes," he assured her, then reached for her once again, sweeping her into his arms to lay her down upon the cool welcoming sand. His arms around her, he kissed her lips passionately, fully, tasting, exploring, demanding, fueling the blaze within him.

His lips left hers, and she stared into his eyes, her lips still slightly open, damp, her breath coming too quickly, the rise of her breasts incredibly seductive in the ethereal glow.

"Now you're supposed to walk away!" she charged him.

He shook his head slowly, eyes roaming over the length of her, from the perfect beauty of her face to the exquisite shape of her hips.

"No," he said hoarsely.

"Maybe I'm supposed to walk away this time," she suggested softly.

Again he shook his head.

"No way—wife. No way."

And then his lips touched hers again.

Chapter 7

She'd felt him behind her, of course, long before he had touched her. His footsteps on the sand had been nearly silent, but she had heard him, sensed him. She had known he was there, standing behind her, watching her, waiting. Thinking.

Thinking what?

That she had come back into his life in a fishnet to spy on him?

No, not at that moment.

At that moment she'd felt the tension, the heat, the electricity. She'd known that they weren't going to argue. That he was going to come closer.

And she hadn't moved.

Somehow she had known that he would touch her again. And some inner voice had shouted, warning her not to trust him.

But she had ached for his touch for too long to be denied now.

No matter what bitterness lay between them, no matter what anger, what distrust... No matter what, when his hands fell upon her flesh, when his lips pressed against her nape, there was something infinitely tender about his touch, as if he were awakening her from some deep sleep. As if she had been waiting all these years.

Perhaps she had been.

Odd, how the sand was suddenly so cool beneath her, hard packed, endlessly white and clean. She saw his eyes above hers, as passionate and determined as his voice had been, their color cobalt in the moonlight, dark with intensity. A great shivering suddenly seized her. The sand was actually cold, the air cool, yet her flesh felt as if it had suddenly caught fire....

Then she felt his lips again. He seemed to kiss her forever, only his mouth touching hers, leaving the rest of her body cold once more, like the sand, waiting, aching, needing more.

Suddenly his lips broke from hers. She was more aware than ever of the chill of the sand beneath her body, and she could hear the surf pounding relentlessly against the beach. She opened her eyes and saw the moon, wondering fleetingly if he hadn't left her again after all, if his anger and bitterness weren't so great that even now he could walk away. An awful anguish filled her, an aching that brought tears to glisten suddenly in her eyes.

Then, without warning, she wasn't cold or empty anymore. He had left her merely to shed his clothes. Now the feel of his hot flesh brought a startling heat and fulfillment as he settled over her, his fingers entwining with hers, his eyes searing hers with dark cobalt fire once again.

"Damn, but it's been a long time," he whispered, the words husky. "A long, long time..."

Eons, she might have whispered. Far too long a time...

But she didn't dare. She didn't dare speak at all, and even if she had wished to, no sound would have come to her lips. She closed her eyes again, aware now of the rough texture of his legs, his chest. Aware of his sex, so hard against her flesh...

He shifted, his knee parting her thighs. Her eyes flew open again, and she saw that he was poised over her, waiting.

Her eyes met his, and then suddenly, shatteringly, he was inside her. Sound at last left her lips, a soft, startled cry that seemed to give him pause until she dug her fingers into his shoulders, arching swiftly against him, taking, wanting, giving, needing to love and to be loved.

The moon seemed to burst, a sudden gleaming splash of color against the dark sky.

Her memory had failed to recall just how wonderful this could be. His touch, his strength, his tenderness. The sheer ecstasy of feeling him gloved within her, moving, igniting a burning, racing fire, a magical heat that filled her and tore through her, spiraling deep to reach her core . . .

No, memory could never serve.

He kissed her lips, her breasts, caressed her, held her. And all the while he moved within her, each thrust bringing her closer and closer to cataclysmic wonder. His hand curved over her buttocks, pressing her even closer to him, driving his thrusts even deeper inside her, touching her within and without. Even in the breeze they both glistened, the sheen of passion gleaming on their bodies, echoing the warmth that burned inside. She scarcely breathed, yet she gasped for breath. She closed her eyes to feel the intensity of the moment, then opened them again and saw the tension in his face, corded in his neck, rippling in his arms. His lips bore down on hers once again; then he stiffened, thrusting so deeply into her that she thought she would die. But she didn't die. Sweet deliciousness seemed to sweep throughout her as fulfillment, wild, volatile and shattering, burst upon her at last. For long moments she was only dimly aware of him, holding her tightly, then quivering with the power of one final thrust before falling to her side.

She shivered suddenly in the chill that raced through her with the warmth of his body gone.

He lay there, too, just breathing.

Then suddenly he sat up, arms clasped round his knees, staring out at the dark surf.

"Damn!" he muttered softly.

She gritted her teeth tightly together, fighting the new wave of hot moisture that rose to her eyes. Three years, then something so sweetly magnificent, and all he had to say was *damn?*

She started to rise. He had already gotten to his feet and reached for his shorts. Now he tossed her the checked midriff top and commanded roughly, "Get dressed."

She caught the blouse, staring at him with a fury so great that she was able to blink away the tears.

"I'd fully intended to dress!" she assured him. "You're the rudest man I've ever—"

The shirt fell to the sand as he suddenly jerked her to her feet. They were both naked in the moon glow, and she felt thoroughly chilled as his eyes bore down into hers.

"The rudest man you've ever *what?*" he demanded. "The rudest man you've ever slept with? Was that it? I imagine Eric is far more polite. Was he at your side like that when he *politely* suggested you dive in the ocean and find out what I knew about the *Contessa?* Did he suggest you go this far?"

"What?" she gasped, unable to believe what she had heard.

She jerked free with a sudden burst of power that surprised even him, then took a swing at him, but he was ready. Yet even as he caught her wrist and dragged her against him, she slammed his chest with her free hand, still struggling fiercely, pitting all her weight against him.

"Little witch," he muttered fiercely, trying to catch her wildly swinging hand, stepping back, hitting a dune—and falling.

They both went tumbling over in the sand, rolling.

Melinda caught herself and tried to struggle up, but he was straddling her.

"Don't you touch me—"

"Melinda—"

"I mean it!" The tears had risen to her eyes again; she couldn't hope to blink them back now.

"Damn it, Melinda, I wish I could believe—"

"I don't give a damn anymore what you believe. Get away from me. Leave me alone!"

He didn't leave her alone. His eyes were as deep and furious as her own, and he didn't budge from his intimate perch atop her.

"Would you like to tell me just what your relationship is with him?" he demanded fiercely.

"No, I would not!" she retorted furiously. "You've decided what it is—I have no intention of telling you a damn thing!"

He sat on his haunches, arms crossed over his chest. She tried to struggle up, but with his legs still locked around her hips, it was impossible.

"I'm going to scream any second," she promised him. "Then I'm going to scratch your eyes out. Then I'm—"

"Longford," he interrupted smoothly.

"I'm going to gouge your chest, and if that doesn't move you, I'm going to bite."

He arched a brow. "How hard and what?" he inquired politely.

"Oh!" She took a swing, but he caught her, leaned low against her.

She spoke through gritted teeth. "I'm really going to hurt you in a minute."

"You really hurt me three years ago," he said softly.

"You walked out."

"You refused to come with me."

She closed her eyes. "I'm going to knock your lights out in about thirty seconds."

He leaned even closer, his chest hair teasing her naked breasts mercilessly. "Not a chance," he assured her.

"Please move!" she grated.

"I want to know about Longford."

"Are you going to believe what I say?" she demanded.

He sat back again, staring at her. She trembled slightly. It was so strange. Three years apart and less than twenty-four hours back together, and now they were arguing naked in the sand.

The naked part was all right.

The things he said were not.

"Look at me," he said very softly. "Meet my eyes. I'll believe anything you say."

She hesitated. Her life really wasn't any of his business. She certainly didn't want to give him any power over her, and she was damn sure *he* hadn't been living her ridiculously celibate life.

But he was determined. Relentless. And perhaps even passionate in his pursuit of what he wanted to know...

"There's nothing between Eric Longford and me," she told him, her eyes steady on his, "other than dinner now and then, a few diving trips, and conversation."

He didn't move. Not for the longest time. His black lashes fell for a moment; then his eyes were hard on hers once again.

"Really?"

"I just told you—"

"Sorry."

"Now, if you'd please—"

"In a minute."

"What?"

"What was that comment about?"

"What comment?" she cried, beginning to feel desperate.

"That I was the rudest man you'd ever slept with."

Anger filled her again, and she gritted her teeth. "You're the densest man I've ever met!" she exclaimed. "I never said that. *Never!* I didn't say the word *slept* at all, and you never gave me a chance to finish the sentence. You're the rudest man I've ever met. *Met!*"

He seemed unaffected by her anger, holding her still. "So who have you been seeing?" he demanded.

"None of your business. And if you don't—"

"Who?" he persisted.

"Let me up!"

"Answer me."

"In about two seconds, I will begin to scream!"

He shrugged. "You won't get a whole lot of help if you do. I have a very loyal crew. Now tell me who, Melinda."

She stared at him, aware of the hard sand beneath her, aware of the power of his thighs and the intimate way they rode her hips. She was aware of the cool air on her body, hardening her nipples, of the very *naked* way he was straddling her...

"No one," she muttered.

"Who?"

"No one!" she lashed out more angrily. "Now will you please—"

"You mean to tell me you haven't...dated seriously? In all this time?"

"If you mean, have I slept with anyone in all this time, the answer is no. Now, damn you, this is supposed to be a barbecue, not *True Confessions!* If you'll please—"

He stood, reaching a hand down to her and drawing her to her feet. She tried to walk by him to retrieve her clothing, but he held onto her wrist, pulling her back.

"So just what were you doing out on the ocean with Longford?"

"Diving."

"And he just left you stranded?"

She sighed. "Yes. I thought the *Crystal Lee* might be yours, and if not, she was someone looking for treasure, not a fishing boat."

"What if she had been a drug runner? What if she hadn't been mine? What if she had belonged to someone ready to slit your throat for getting in his way?"

"I can take care of myself."

He groaned. "Right. Just dive into a fishing net. Age isn't doing a damn thing for your common sense."

"And it hasn't improved your manners."

"Your recklessness—"

"Isn't your concern!"

"Actually, it is," he said softly, releasing her at last as his eyes met hers with cool speculation. "It seems that until we manage to do something about it, you're still my wife."

"Don't let it concern you."

"But it does." His eyes dropped to study the length of her, causing a rush of blood to bring a crimson tide to her flesh.

His eyes met hers again. "We'd really better get dressed. My crew may be around any minute now."

"Would they follow their great leader if he'd given the impression he was out for privacy?" she mocked.

He shrugged. "By now, they may think the sharks have already eaten us both. Get your things on. Someone might be along any second."

She turned away from him, quickly picking up the few pieces of her clothing and shimmying into them. She didn't look his way.

When she did, he was clad in his shorts once again and walking the way he had come, calling over his shoulder, "I'm sure dinner is on. Let's go back."

"Maybe I'd rather go for a swim!" she retorted.

Then she made the mistake of turning away from him.

Footsteps came pounding toward her. He could run as fleetly as he could swim. She found herself gasping for breath as he swept her off her feet and into his arms. "No night swimming alone, you little idiot. Damn it. You are the most headstrong and reckless female I have ever—"

"Slept with?" she suggested.

He was silent for a second. Then a slow grin curved his lip. "I was going to say *met!*" he informed her.

He started walking back along the beach. For a moment Melinda let herself be carried. It was nice. So nice.

Then she looked up at him, determined. "So who are *you* sleeping with these days?" she asked, trying to keep her tone light.

He looked down at her, mischief burning in his eyes. "None of your business," he said softly.

She stiffened. "You hairy son of a sea serpent!" she cried angrily, shoving at his chest until he half set her down, half dropped her.

"Hey!" He caught her arm when she would have run past him.

She faced him, her hands tightening into fists at her side. "You sat there and forced me to tell you all about my life, and now you tell me that yours is none of my business?"

He cocked his head, thinking for a moment. Then he shrugged. "That's right," he told her. And he was the one to walk away then.

She ran after him. "Roc, you bas—" she began, but his finger fell on her lips.

His eyes were intense and his voice husky when he promised her softly, "I'll tell you this. I have never, never slept with anyone like you in all my life. Never. Now, come on—Ms. Davenport."

She spun around quickly, startled by the effect his words had on her. Once again, she was just a breath away from tears. She was in better shape when he was being rude, when he was angry, making demands!

She walked quickly, keeping several feet in front of him. When she finally saw his crew, Connie was anxiously pacing before the fire, Marina staring into it, and Joe, Peter and Bruce were looking in the direction from which she and Roc were coming.

Guilt plagued her. They were all worried. And wondering, of course, if they should be saving their leader—or leaving him to his, er, private recreation.

Connie stopped pacing. The three men tried to look in different directions.

"Something smells wonderful!" Melinda called out, only a slight tremor in her voice. Dear lord. She could feel crimson color flooding her face again. Did everyone know exactly what she had been doing?

Roc was closer behind her than she had suspected. She nearly jumped when he said, "Well, did you all start eating yet? What are we waiting for? Connie, is there a cold beer for me?"

"Sure!" Connie called. "We—uh, yeah, well, we kind of waited. The fish was too tempting, though. Marina's got more. We'll put it right on."

Roc shook his head, accepting the beer Connie handed him. "The chicken's fine for me."

"For me, too," Melinda echoed quickly.

"There's plenty more," Marina offered, her dark eyes giving away no hint of curiosity.

"We'll have it another time," Melinda promised, trying to sound cheerful.

"Catch!" Roc called suddenly, throwing her a can of beer. She caught it swiftly, wondering just what Roc had told these people about her.

They'd definitely known he'd had a wife. And that she was old man Davenport's daughter.

They'd all been wary enough of her, certainly.

The barbecue was delicious, and the night was beautiful. One by one everyone came to sit around the fire. The orange flames snapped and crackled against the ever-darkening night.

Roc was across from her. She was half listening to one of Bruce's tales about a ghost ship that sailed the Atlantic when, in the very middle of the story, she found herself distracted again with an inner trembling.

How could she be sitting here so calmly when they had made love in the sand such a little while ago? When he had accused her of such awful things, when he had nearly walked away, when he had made her tell him everything.

She was a fool.

She could still close her eyes and feel his touch. . . .

And, looking across the fire, she could see his shoulders glinting copper in the fire glow, see his eyes, which met hers now and then, still questioning.

She had told him the truth, yet he still seemed suspicious.

"Oh!" Connie gasped, letting out a little scream and jumping up.

A branch had fallen where she had been sitting. A very small one.

Bruce burst out laughing. "Connie!" he admonished his sister.

"Well, it scared me!" she snapped. She stared at her brother, shaking a firm finger at him. "You were sitting there talking about bony fingers and suddenly—" She broke off. "Where did that branch come from?" she asked, frowning.

Melinda turned around. The trees were some distance away.

Peter stood, as well, shrugging. "The wind must have carried it from those trees over there."

Connie shivered, staring at them. "Bony fingers, dead eyes!" she muttered. "It's like they're looking at us, isn't it?"

Roc moved to stand behind Connie, staring off at the trees, too.

"You feel eyes in the darkness?" he asked, but his tone wasn't as light as Bruce's. Melinda stared at him, wondering what he could possibly be thinking.

"It's late," Connie murmured.

"Very late," Marina agreed, rising and immediately and efficiently beginning to gather up the dinner things.

Without comment, the others began to help her. Melinda gathered the utensils, while Roc and Peter made sure the fire was completely out. With very little conversation, everything was gathered and brought to the dinghy.

The same efficiency made cleanup equally quick when they returned to the *Crystal Lee.*

When they'd finished, Marina told Melinda goodnight and left her in the galley.

Alone, Melinda hesitated, then climbed to the deck. She could hear Roc discussing the next day's dive with Peter and Bruce.

She didn't feel like seeing them all again, so she hurried silently to the captain's cabin.

She hesitated for a long time, then stripped and hopped in the shower, washing away the sand that still clung to her.

When she came out of the shower, the cabin was still empty. She hesitated again, then turned off the light on the desk, crawled into the captain's bunk and lay there listening to the cacophony of her own heart.

Minutes later, the door to the cabin opened. Moonlight filtered in, and she saw Roc silhouetted there, the light gleaming on his shoulders, his face in shadows.

His thoughts in darkness.

Then he entered the cabin, closing the door behind him, moving like a cat in the night, silent, graceful.

She nearly gasped when she realized that he was standing by her side.

"Sleeping?" he asked softly.

She shook her head, then wondered if he saw the motion. "No."

"You've waited up?"

"I—I showered. The sand, you know."

"Umm. The sand. I haven't showered. Should I?"

She felt her heart slamming again. "Your life is none of my business, remember?"

"So I shouldn't shower?"

She smiled suddenly, her lashes sweeping her cheeks. "It's entirely up to you."

"Ah. So I'm not welcome."

She scooted over toward the paneling, running her hand over the empty expanse beside her.

"No," she said very softly, "you're very welcome—with or without sand."

They were the last words she spoke that night. In a matter of seconds he was stretched beside her, warm, electric.

And the sand didn't matter in the least.

Chapter 8

The next day they explored the same area again. Melinda seemed drawn to it, Roc realized, and though they still hadn't found anything, he was more than willing to go with her instincts.

So far, she'd found the only real clue to the *Contessa.*

She was ahead of him today, moving with tremendous ease and grace before him in the fascinating if sometimes eerie world of the sea. The coral shelf to their left housed a wild variety of creatures. Huge, slow groupers—two of them, maybe four hundred pounds apiece—were staring at them with glassy eyes. Just beyond the big fish there was a plateau of anemones, with pretty, bright orange and white clownfish—tiny as fingertips—darting swiftly within their hosts' wavy fingers, luring prey for the anemone that supported the fish.

They passed a pair of yellow tangs, brighter than sunlight. Yet even as they passed the tiny creatures, Roc suddenly became aware of something much larger looming in the water.

Instinctive wariness held him still as he watched, but experience told him the creature wasn't a shark. Just ahead of him, Melinda, too, had gone still, watching, waiting.

Then the creature came into full view, and Roc grinned around his mouthpiece. They were being visited by a dolphin.

That the curious mammal was swimming near them was not an unusual experience. Dolphins were common in these waters—both the mammal, like their friendly visitors, and also the very edible, much smaller and brightly colored dolphin *fish*—but as often as Roc had seen them swimming near him before, he had never seen one behave quite like this. The animal swam straight to Melinda.

He saw her eyes widen behind her mask. She arched a brow to him, then reached out.

Just like a puppy or a kitten, the dolphin seemed to want to be scratched.

Melinda's hand moved gently, knuckles stroking down the creature's throat and downward to its belly. Her air bubbles rose around them both. The dolphin arched its body and plummeted in a smooth dive beneath Melinda. Roc swung around just in time for it to come up on his other side, staring at him with dark eyes, like a precocious youngster who had managed to trick his parents.

He'd swum with dolphins before, having studied them as part of his major in school. They were, in his opinion, absolutely incredible creatures, amazingly intelligent and definitely capable of affection. In captivity, those individuals born and raised with human interaction could display a startling ability to form friendships with man. But in all his days of diving on the ocean floor, he'd never seen one come quite so trustingly close in the wild as this fellow was doing.

He wondered if perhaps the animal hadn't belonged to an aquarium or private study facility, then somehow found its way to the ocean, because it wasn't just being friendly, it wanted to move right in.

Roc reached out a hand, too, touching the dolphin. It edged closer to him, accepting his touch, moving just as if it wanted to be scratched once again, like a cat curling up on its master's lap before a roaring fire.

Melinda swam around, fascinated, running her hand down the dolphin's back once again.

Roc motioned her to move on, curious to see what the dolphin would do.

It followed them.

They spent several minutes swimming around the edge of the World War Two wreck again, crossing through skeleton doorways, over chunks of metal long grown over with seaweed and coral, their new friend following them.

It was a fascinating dive, but one that was yielding nothing, Roc decided wearily a few minutes later as he checked his watch.

He caught up with Melinda and tapped on his dial to show her they were running out of time. She seemed surprised and looked as if she were about to move onward again. He shook his head.

She nodded, and they started toward the ship, the newfound friend still following them.

As they neared the *Crystal Lee,* Melinda paused again, stroking the dolphin. She stared at Roc, and he could see her smiling around her mouthpiece. He shrugged. The dolphin swam around them again, and he reached out, stroking it. Then he gave the water a flippered kick that brought him to the surface, where he spat out his mouthpiece and swam the fifteen feet that brought him to the ladder at the back of the boat. Wrenching off his flippers, he crawled aboard. Bruce was there instantly, taking his tanks and mask as he slid them off.

"Well?" Bruce said anxiously.

Roc shook his head, watching for Melinda. If she was staying down to play with that dolphin...

But just then she broke the surface, quickly swimming toward the boat, reaching the ladder, shedding her flippers, crawling aboard. She ripped off her mask as Roc caught her tanks.

"It was wonderful!" she cried excitedly.

"You did find something!" Bruce exclaimed.

"A dolphin!" Melinda replied, happily nodding her head.

Bruce frowned instantly, staring at Roc. "A dolphin?" he whispered, deflated.

"It was wonderful!" Melinda repeated.

Bruce looked at her as if he wondered what she had been breathing out of her tanks. "But, Melinda, there are lots of dolphins in this area. You must have seen them before."

She sat on the edge of the boat, squeezing the water out of her hair, shaking her head. "Bruce, never in my whole life have I seen one like this. Tell him, Roc!"

A smile curved his lips, and startling warmth swept over him, a tenderness. Her enthusiasm was contagious, her fascinated pleasure with the creature something so warm and real that he found himself wanting to sweep her into his arms then and there.

He leaned back instead, arms crossed over his chest, and shrugged. "I think our friend below must have had human contact before. Perhaps he belonged to an aquarium or private researchers. He is—" He paused a moment, looking over at Melinda; then he grinned. "He is pretty wonderful."

Just as he finished speaking, Joe and Marina, who had also been diving, broke the surface behind them, coming aboard.

"Eh, mon! You never seen such a fish!" Joe exclaimed, coming aboard. "He thought he was my poodle!"

Melinda laughed, staring at Bruce. "See!" she charged.

With the Tobagos aboard, Connie came hurrying out of the galley, and they were all together at the bow of the boat, Connie and Bruce listening to the others' tale about the dolphin.

"I'd love to see him!" Connie exclaimed.

"He'll probably swim around again," Bruce said.

"But maybe he won't," Connie worried.

"He may already be gone," Roc warned.

"I'll go see," Melinda volunteered quickly. She stood, poised to dive off the edge of the boat. Roc told himself that he really had no right to stop her. She wasn't wearing a mask, fins or a tank, but she didn't need them for what she wanted to do. If the dolphin was around, it would play with her right on the surface.

She arched a brow at him, a small smile curving her lips. An invitation.

He shrugged, then leaped up with her. His fingers curled around hers, and they jumped from the bow together, plummeting swiftly downward into the temperate waters.

It was there—their new mascot—the dolphin waiting just as if it had known that they would come back to play with it.

Melinda caught hold of its dorsal fin, and the creature took her for a swift ride, striking out away from the boat, then swiftly turning and bringing her right back to where they had started from. She grinned at

Roc, blinking against the salt in the water, then jack-knifed her legs to bring her to the surface for air.

He followed her. With both their heads breaking the surface, Melinda shouted to Connie, "Come on down! He's here!"

"Bruce, please, let's go see it. We've got enough tanks."

Bruce grumbled, but he was already getting the tanks that would allow himself and his sister to dive. Treading water now, Roc called out to Melinda, ten feet away, "Okay, Ms. Davenport, can we let the others play with your sea beast now? We're turning into raisins here."

She hesitated, as if she were about to protest, then lowered her lashes swiftly and agreed.

Funny behavior for Melinda. She'd been with him for three days.

With two incredible nights between them now...

And she'd been an angel, never disagreeing with a single captain's command.

"Why are you staring at me like that?" she demanded.

"I'm wondering what you're up to," he called honestly.

A flash of fire touched her eyes, but she didn't reply; instead she swam to the boat, crawling aboard easily, even as Connie toppled smoothly backward over the edge, wearing her gear.

Roc followed, but more slowly. When he crawled aboard the boat, she had already disappeared. Joe and

Marina were still seated on the bow, discussing the extraordinary behavior of the dolphin. Roc caught Joe's eyes, and he knew his friend instantly realized that he was wondering where his wife had disappeared to so quickly.

"She said she had a chill, boss man!" Joe said softly, a slightly wicked gleam in his dark eyes. "She needed a warm shower and a hot cup of coffee."

Roc nodded, staring at Joe warily, sliding down beside Marina. So she had a chill. Great. He'd just had to say something to ruin things when they were going incredibly well....

But why?

He was startled by the swift pain that seemed to seize him, just like a knife in the chest. It was frightening. And he hated like hell to admit fear. But Melinda was here. Spending her days with him.

Spending her nights with him.

And in those days and nights, it was so easy to go back, to pretend they had never been apart. There were even moments when he could forget that his wife had chosen her father over her husband....

Then there would be those other moments, moments when he would wonder what she was doing there. She had, after all, more or less leaped aboard from Eric Longford's boat, and her father was still Jonathan Davenport.

She had definitely been stunned to discover that she was still legally married to him, and yet...

There were the nights.

He did seem to have the good sense to keep his mouth shut when they were in bed together, but at other times, the bitterness remained. The mistrust. And then he just had to ask what she was doing here. They were on a treasure hunt. He needed to be on the alert. Yet every moment he was near her, his guard relaxed a little bit.

So there was the possibility that she could be sleeping with him by night, searching with him by day... and radioing to her father during any private moment she might be able to sneak!

Well, the future remained to be seen. And if he hurt her with his suspicions, then he was sorry, but then she damned well deserved them.

He realized that Joe and Marina were staring at him, and he scowled.

"My friend," Joe said softly, "I suggest we go ashore for a break."

"A break!"

"We need supplies," Marina told him. "We're nearly out of sugar and coffee and detergent."

"We're low on gas," Joe added.

"And," Marina added, "a night in Nassau might do us all good. Dinner at a restaurant."

"Dancing," Joe added.

Roc sat back, lifting his hands, then letting them fall again. "We're on the brink of discovery—" he began.

"And growing more and more frustrated every day," Joe reminded him. "We know we're in the right place. We're staring straight at the answer—we just haven't touched it yet. Maybe we need to close our eyes, take a break and look again."

Roc started to protest again, but he fell silent instead. Frowning, he thought over Joe's words. Maybe his friend was right. They were staring at the answer. They couldn't see it. Maybe they needed to look away.

"All right," he said quietly. "It should be about two hours into Nassau Harbor. We'll go for tonight—we'll leave by ten tomorrow morning. Marina, that will give you time for shopping and a little R and R."

Marina smiled. "Plenty of time."

"I think—" Roc began, and then he broke off.

"You think what?" Joe asked.

Roc shook his head.

Melinda.

Bring me to a port, any port, she had told him. But she had been determined to come aboard his boat, and now she had even been diving with him, and he would be damned if she was going to get the chance to rejoin her father and dive these waters with him.

Or with Eric Longford.

"I think I need a cup of coffee myself," he said, and stood, then strode toward the steps that led to the galley.

The breeze and sun had dried him by then, and he hurried downward in his damp trunks and bare feet.

Melinda wasn't in the galley.

He strode to the stove and poured himself a cup of coffee, quickly swallowing a sip of the hot black liquid. He swallowed more, wondering what would happen when he reached New Providence, Nassau Harbor, and let his wife reach civilization and a telephone.

And access to the world, if she chose...

He crossed the galley and left it behind, coming to the main deck and swiftly dispensing with the fifteen feet to his own cabin. He threw the door open and entered, closing the door behind him.

Melinda was sitting on the bunk, clad in a white terry robe, towel drying her hair, which she had evidently just washed. She smelled clean, redolent of fresh soap and shampoo. With her hair sleek and wet and pulled back, her eyes were startling against the golden tan of her face.

She stared at him as he entered, watched him warily as he crossed the room and sat on the opposite end of the bunk, leaning against the wall.

"What?" she asked at last, an edge to her voice.

"What are you doing here?" he asked her.

Her lashes fell over her eyes. When they rose again, their aquamarine depths were blazing.

"Sleeping with you for all your deep, dark secrets!" she snapped.

He reached for her, catching her wrists, drawing her close, causing the brush to fall from her fingers. She didn't protest, didn't fight him or say a word. Her chin remained high, her shoulders straight—her eyes afire.

"Damn you, Melinda."

"Isn't that the answer you want?" she demanded.

"I want the truth!" he shouted; then he gritted his teeth, aware of how loud he had been and equally aware that he didn't want anyone else knowing his affairs.

She pulled free of his hold, rising, walking across the cabin as if she had to keep her distance from him. "It doesn't matter what I say to you now," she told him. "I keep thinking that it does, and I even think that whatever the future brings, these days have been . . . worth the price. Then I look at you, and before you even speak I see it all in your eyes—I've just come to get whatever information I can and bring it back to my father. And Eric."

Her words were so cool, so controlled. He liked her anger better. At least there was passion in it, emotion, a link between them that erupted into more.

He hated her words. He wanted to dispute them.

But they were true.

He stood and walked across the cabin to her, opening his mouth to speak. It would have been easier if she hadn't smelled so delicious. If he hadn't hungered for her for so long. If he didn't know that she was naked beneath the robe, and if he didn't know just how sweet and tempting and stunning that nakedness would be . . .

"No!" she whispered suddenly, backing away from him. He was amazed to see the glaze of tears in her eyes, when she had been so cold. . . .

"No what?" he demanded.

She shook her head. "I know...I know that look in your eyes," she murmured as her lashes fell, and against her tan there was a sudden touch of rose. "And it's not..."

"Not what?"

She shook her head again. "You can't do this!" she whispered frantically. "You can't accuse me of everything in the world and then decide that none of it matters if you want to..."

"Make love," he finished roughly. He wanted to push her away, but even more than that he wanted to sweep her into his arms. He threw his hands up in the air. "Damn you!" he whispered. Then he repeated it again raggedly, "Damn you! I can't help it, Melinda, what do you want from me? You chose another man over me—"

"My father—"

"It doesn't matter—you were my wife!"

She swung around, turning her back on him.

He watched her for a moment, aching to touch her, but somehow he managed not to.

"Well," he said softly. "The ball is going to be in your court, Ms. Davenport. We're spending the night in Nassau."

She swung around, staring at him. "What?"

"We're spending the night in Nassau. Of course, if you do disappear and find your way to your father—or Longford—I will manage to find you and wring your neck."

"By what right—"

"You're still my wife!"

She started to walk past him, heading for the cabin door, her strides determined. He caught her arm.

"Let me go," she demanded, her eyes wild.

"I don't think so."

"I don't need to be near you and your—"

"Why are you here, Melinda?"

She jerked away from him. The glaze of tears was in her eyes again. "Has it ever occurred to you that the entire world isn't black and white, Captain Trellyn? Maybe my father was wrong, maybe he even hedged the truth with me—"

"Lied."

"All right, damn you, maybe he lied. He was wrong, he didn't do something that was great, but his transgression against you didn't turn him into a dangerous and evil man!"

"What are you saying to me?"

"Maybe I was wrong, maybe he was wrong, maybe you were wronged. But you weren't perfect in all that happened, either. You walked in and asked me to turn my back on my father—"

"He was wrong!"

"He was still my father!" she cried.

His fingers were wound so tightly around her wrists that he was surprised she didn't cry out. He forced himself to ease his hold. "So why are you here?" he demanded.

"Because we were *wrong!*" she cried in exasperation, trying with no success to free herself from his touch. Her head flew back, her eyes a sea of blue-green fire once again. "Because on this one," she gasped, "I figured I owed you. I wanted you to make this claim. I wanted you to find your *Contessa.*"

She trembled with the passion of her words, with the fury of them, with the emotion of them. He tried to stiffen his shoulders, tried to retain rational thought. It was all drifting away in his hunger to slip his hands over her bare shoulders, to force the terry robe to fall to the floor. But his fingers were trembling as he held her, and he gritted his teeth hard.

"So, Ms. Davenport, when I pull into Nassau, you'll be staying with me? My wife, in my room?"

"Yes, your wife!" she snapped out. "But you don't even call me by my name anymore, it's always *Ms. Davenport!*"

Startled, he nearly stepped back. He *had* been calling her Ms. Davenport almost continually since she had come aboard. Maybe it had been a defense mechanism, part of the wall he had erected against her. But now . . .

Now it surprised him that she had noticed, and that it had apparently bothered her.

Anger drained from him as he stared at her taut, strained features and dazzling eyes.

"All right, Mrs. Trellyn," he said very softly, "when I pull into Nassau, are you sharing a room with me? Perhaps dinner and dancing ashore? Or will you be leaving at the first opportunity?"

Her lashes fell swiftly.

"Melinda!"

Her eyes rose to his again. "Yes!" she hissed.

"Yes, *which?*" he demanded hoarsely.

"I'll be staying with you!" she cried angrily. Her lower lip was trembling. "I told you, I'm here to see that you make your claim, that . . ."

Her voice trailed away, but it didn't matter. He set his forefinger on the trembling curve of her lower lip and stared at it, fascinated.

Then, at long last, he gave in to temptation, slipping his hands beneath the terry robe to her bare shoulders, touching the smoothness of her skin, causing the robe to fall to the floor. He moved his finger so that his lips could touch down on hers, then cradled her in his arms, kissing her passionately.

For one brief moment, she was stiff. Resisting him . . .

Then her arms curled around his neck, and he threaded his fingers through the drying strands of golden hair that waved over her shoulders, entangling them both. She was flush against his body, the tips of her breasts hardened cherry peaks against the dark hair on his chest. He groaned aloud, kissing her, tasting her, feeling the fullness of her lithe form against his, feeling the desperate rise of heat and hardness within himself.

Her lips broke from his suddenly, her fingers trailing over his shoulders as her mouth touched the furiously pounding pulse at his throat. She lowered herself against him, lips, teeth and tongue playing over his chest, fingers rubbing his muscled flesh, his nipples, the lines of his ribs. She followed the curve of his body still lower; then her fingers were around the elastic rim of his trunks, sliding them down over his hips. He stepped instantly from them, kicking them aside.

She dropped suddenly on her knees before him, and he gasped with the shattering sensation that filled him like lightning when she took him in her hands, stroking, touching him.

Lowering her golden blond head, she stroked him anew.

The world exploded, or perhaps it was only himself. He bent down, sweeping her up, his lips covering hers as he carried her swiftly to the bunk, setting her there, straddling her, then lying at her side, the pulse that had guided him before now beating a thousand times harder, pounding within his head, his heart, his loins.

His mouth found hers again. Left it. Touched down upon a very delicate vein at her throat. His eyes met hers again. They seemed so liquid, so beautiful, so mesmerizing.

"I..." she whispered.

"Yes?" he demanded huskily.

Her eyes closed against him. "Want you," she said very softly.

"Well, *Mrs. Trellyn,* you've got me!" he assured her huskily.

Indeed, she had him....

He stared over the length of her. The slim, shapely, so damned perfect length of her. His hands covered her breasts, encircling them. His head lowered, and he tasted the tips with his tongue, cherished their fullness with fiery liquid caresses. Her fingers dug into his hair, danced slowly over his back, dug again as she groaned softly, shifting beneath him.

He spread his hand over her abdomen, seeing the bronze of his skin against the pale flesh that was normally covered by her bathing suit. He pressed his lips there. Circled his tongue around her navel. Inched downward against her, watching his fingers as they entered the golden blond triangle above her thighs. Felt her move and shift and writhe beneath him.

He shifted his own weight up, parting her thighs fluidly, his knees between them. Then he lowered his head, stroking and touching and laving with a searing, wet, intimate desire.

She shuddered, gasped, cried out. He rose above her, taking her into his arms, sinking deeply within her until she shuddered anew, all the while whispering her name....

Minutes later, hours, moments—he didn't know which—the whole of the world seemed to explode again. She trembled wickedly within his arms; then they drifted to earth, and her trembling became shivers as the cool afternoon air settled over bodies that had burned and now grew chill. He held her close, tenderly, neither of them speaking for the longest time.

Then he realized that she was staring at the paneled ceiling above them. He stroked her cheek, and she turned toward him, her eyes damp.

"What is it?" he asked her softly.

She shook her head.

"Melinda?"

"I..."

"What?"

Her lips moved; and she shook her head again, her lashes falling quickly over her eyes. "I swear," she murmured. "I want to help you stake your claim."

Silently he cradled her against him once again. He stroked her hair and felt the rocking of the boat.

Then he groaned.

"What?" she asked him softly.

"Well, if we're going to make Nassau tonight, I'd better get moving."

He rose. She curled his pillow to her chest, staring at him with a troubled gaze.

"Why are we going to Nassau?"

"Marina needs some supplies. And she also thinks we can't see the forest for the trees."

Melinda nodded, understanding with no more need for an explanation.

"I'm going to shower," he told her.

She nodded again. He started toward the head door, wishing he could stay in the bunk with her.

Yet suddenly more anxious than ever to reach Nassau. A luxury hotel room for the night. A great dinner somewhere, and then the night ahead of them. In an air-conditioned room, maybe with a bottle of champagne at their side . . .

"Roc!" she called after him.

He paused, turning. She half rose, watching him with eyes that had gone dark with emotion again, tense, passionate.

"I meant what I said. I told you the truth. I want *you* to make this claim."

He walked to her and kissed the top of her head, then looked into her eyes again.

"You know what I want?" he asked her softly.

She shook her head, and he kissed her lips lightly.

"Well, I very much want you to be *Mrs. Trellyn* tonight," he told her.

She searched his eyes.

"Well," she murmured lightly. "It seems you've got me."

So it seemed. . . .

He managed to turn around again, and this time he made it to the shower.

After all, the night loomed ahead. . . .

Chapter 9

The first time Melinda had entered Nassau Harbor, she had felt a strange affinity and affection for the place. She'd been a little girl that first time, spending the summer with her father. The summers had been magical times to begin with. The year had always seemed so hard, so strained. She loved her mother, but she never really knew her, so she would sit throughout the year dreaming about the summer, about sailing on her father's boats, racing the wind, or motoring through the waves on one quest or another, but always following the lure of adventure. He had brought her to many of the islands in the Bahamas, the heavily populated ones, the not-so-populated ones, even the uninhabited ones. She had learned very early to love the tranquil azure waters, the gentle, laid-back singsong of the people, the sun that shone so frequently and so fiercely, the magical beaches and the lure of the reefs. She loved so many of the islands. But sometimes, she thought, coming here was the best of all.

Nassau, the hub of the Bahamian island of New Providence, was definitely filled with tourists and tourist attractions, but it always seemed to carry a little bit of the past with it, a charming past, filled with the nice and the not so nice, but even the shadowy realms of the past seemed to add to the draw of the place. In her day, Nassau had been a haven for countless pirates. She had harbored smugglers, thieves, murderers and more, and she had survived them all.

Coming in was always beautiful. Giant cruise ships often lingered in the harbor while their passengers were off motorcycling or shopping, visiting forts, or sitting in quaint little restaurants for tea. In the downtown section many of the buildings were from the colonial period, painted in soft pastels that seemed to beckon the traveler from the sea.

It was a comfortable place for American citizens, with easy customs procedures, and Roc dropped her and all the crew except for Joe Tobago on the dock to acquire rooms for the evening while he cleared the *Crystal Lee* for the night and made provisions to obtain gas and a few other necessities for the boat.

Marina, with relatives in town, shooed Melinda, Bruce and Connie on to check in to the hotel they had chosen, telling them that she was going shopping for bargains, and that she and Joe would see them at dinner.

"Let's walk along Bay Street a little bit," Connie suggested as they stood on the dock.

Bruce groaned.

"All right," Melinda quickly agreed.

"How about I go get rooms, and you two go walking?" Joe suggested.

Connie grinned. "Great!" she told her brother.

So she and Melinda did just that, jostling with the tourists through the straw market, where Connie found a new hat for the endless days on the *Crystal Lee* with the sun beating down, and then they wandered past hawkers with their wares to Bay Street, where the shops were indoors, often air-conditioned, and offered many exotic and expensive perfumes and imported wools and clothing, as well as more touristy goods.

Melinda waved a perfume bottle beneath her nose in one store and discovered Connie behind her, sniffing as well. "That's wonderful! What is it?"

"Something native, I think. Umm, here. They call it Passion Flower," Melinda told her.

Connie picked up the vial, then surveyed the shelf. "They have bath oil, perfume, dusting powder . . . the works." She picked up Melinda's wrist where Melinda had dabbed the perfume. "Oh, wow, this smells great on you."

Melinda shrugged. "I'm just window-shopping," she told Connie.

"But it's—" Connie began, but she stopped short. "Oh, I know. You don't have your wallet, But I have mine—"

"Connie, I'm not going to borrow money from you."

"But I have one of your husband's credit cards."

Melinda's brows shot up in surprise. Connie shrugged and explained quickly. "We all have them. He's extraordinary to work for. He's great about giving credit to everyone, about sharing all our finds—and he still covers expenses. None of us abuse the privilege, you know—"

"Connie, I can't imagine you abusing anything!" Melinda assured the pretty blonde quickly.

"This perfume is great. And you should get it. Let me put it on his card."

Melinda shook her head. "No."

"He's your husband—"

Melinda shook her head emphatically. "Connie, honestly, neither one of us knew it, so it doesn't count."

Connie grinned suddenly. "You know, you're not half the shrew you're supposed to be. Not that Roc ever said anything about you, you know. But we all kind of knew the story. And I didn't mean that. About being half a shrew. You're not a shrew at all, but even other divers are kind of in awe of your abilities, and I guess men think a woman has to be tough and—oh, wow, I'm not getting myself out of this at all, am I?"

Melinda, grinning, shook her head.

"I'm buying a pack of this stuff, from the soap and bubble bath on down."

"Not for me."

"For you. On your husband's credit card."

"But—"

"Well, you are sleeping with him again, aren't you?" Connie demanded.

This was absurd. She felt like laughing while she turned every color of crimson, also while turning swiftly around to see just who else might have heard Connie's question.

"Connie—"

"Trust me! He won't mind."

There was no stopping the woman. Melinda stayed with her to make sure she didn't buy out the store; then they left, and in the next shop Connie found a bikini she thought would be perfect for Melinda. She also insisted that Melinda couldn't keep diving in the same bathing suit over and over again, so in the end, Connie bought the suit, but Melinda insisted that she would pay her back just as soon as she got hold of some of her own money.

"Roc pays really well—"

"So does my father!" Melinda assured her.

They spent another hour poking around as if they were tourists. Melinda discovered that though Connie had been to Nassau a dozen times, she'd never managed to hear much of its history, so Melinda told her about the wild pirate days. The island had been in bad shape when Woodes Rogers, the first royal governor of the Bahamas, arrived in Nassau in 1718, determined to make it a decent place to live. He was so determined that he made the pirates clean up the island, even managing to make a few of them clean up themselves.

They wandered past some of the beautiful buildings from the late 1700s, and Melinda told her that many of the American colonists who had been loyal to Great Britain during the Revolutionary War had hurried here once their cause had been lost. At last they turned toward their hotel.

Bruce met them in the lobby. He'd already showered and shaved and settled in, so it seemed, and he was just waiting to give them their keys before moving out to the terrace for a few drinks beneath the coolness of the ceiling fans. Connie promised to join him shortly, and Bruce shrugged. "We've got dinner reservations in the Turtle Room for eight. Just be there," he warned.

Melinda and Connie left Bruce in the lobby, then parted from each other in the elevator. Connie got off on the second floor, and as the elevator took her up to the seventh floor—the highest—Melinda mused at Roc's choice. He tended to like things that were old and atmospheric, but this was one of the new hotels, beautiful but modern.

When she turned her key in the door and entered her room, she paused, biting her lip, all at once understanding his choice.

The room was heaven.

Huge windows overlooked the harbor and the beautiful old buildings, the whole bustle of the place. There was a door to her left leading to a spacious bathroom, and the king-size bed was to the right of the magnificent windows, while there was a huge Jacuzzi to the left of them. A wet bar flanked the rear wall, while a large-screen TV and video system was set across from the bed.

"Wow!" she murmured softly.

She dropped her duffel bag of borrowed belongings and walked over to the tub, reading the instructions on how to use it. It was wonderfully tempting. She set the water and the temperature, then brought over a few of the Passion Flower bubble cubes. She was just about to strip and plunge in when there was a soft knock on the door.

She opened it to find a bellman there with a package for her.

"There must be a mistake—" she began.

"No, ma'am. Your husband sent this. There's a card."

"Oh!" she murmured. Where was Roc? And what was he up to now? She felt a too familiar trembling seize hold of her. Some moments could be so perfect. So unbelievably perfect. Then she would see his eyes on her, see the suspicion in them, and she would wonder—no, she would know!—that he doubted her again, and her heart would sink, because she was so afraid that he could never really trust her again.

"Oh," she said again, taking the package from the man. "I'm so sorry," she said awkwardly, "I don't have a cent on me at the moment. If you'll give me your name—"

"I'm all taken care of, lady," he assured her swiftly, with a wide smile. "Enjoy."

She closed the door, studying the package. Then she walked to the bed and ripped the paper off with a burning curiosity.

It was a dress. The fabric was a wild mixture of exotic colors, turquoises and blues and greens, fashioned into a strapless creation with a short flared skirt. It was made of the softest silk, with a petticoat to go under the skirt. There were also a number of skimpy silk panties in the bundle, and a pair of white sandals.

And a note.

Size 7 on the dress, 8 on the shoes. I'm sure memory serves me correctly. Please accept these, as I'm anxious for Mrs. Trellyn to appear tonight in her own clothing, and they are offered with all good heart. See you soon, Roc.

Melinda set the package down softly, her fingers moving over the cool silk. It was a beautiful dress, and it would be perfect for her. He'd always had an eye for clothing.

"Offered with all good heart..." she whispered aloud. "And what do you think that means?" she asked the dress. "I'm not after a present—I'm after a lifetime!"

She set the dress down, certain that it wasn't proper to accept such a present from a husband she had just discovered was still hers.

Or was he?

She clenched her teeth tightly, wondering if she wanted a relationship that was constantly embittered by suspicion and feeling a moment's desolation as she wondered if there could possibly be any way back.

Yet that afternoon . . .

Things could be so wonderful. Maybe she did have a chance. She'd tried so hard not to respond to many of his comments. Just as she'd tried so hard that afternoon not to let the words slip from her lips. *I love you . . .*

She had been so close to whispering them, so close to giving away the truth—along with her heart, her soul and her pride. It had to wait, she knew. Had to wait until he believed in her again.

Until maybe he could fall in love with her again. She'd revealed a great deal about how she'd spent the time they'd been apart from one another—and he hadn't told her a thing.

She sat at the foot of the bed, feeling overwhelmed for a moment. Then she looked at the tub, filled with Passion Flower bubbles, and she stripped off her shorts and shirt and stepped in.

The water was hot. She winced, then felt the steam crawl all over her. It was a delicious, soothing feeling. She sank down, closed her eyes and appreciated the sheer physical comfort, then opened her eyes again and appreciated the size of the tub. It was oval, surrounded by beautiful tile and handsome brass racks for towels and robes, and small brass shelves for soaps and shampoos. The bubbles broke around her, their sweet scent rising to her.

Please, God, she thought suddenly, don't let me fail him. She closed her eyes, thinking again of the night when he had left, how she had been so certain that he wouldn't go....

Her father had told her within a few weeks that he had colored the truth a little and that she should give Roc a call.

She'd been so hurt then. Devastated. And determined that no one would know.

Then again, what she had said today had been the truth. Her father had behaved badly, though he wasn't a bad man. He had loved Roc like a son, taken him beneath his wing.

"Stubborn!" she said softly.

She closed her eyes again, savoring the heat. Then she heard a key twisting in the lock, and she looked up quickly. The door opened and closed.

Roc was there.

He strode in, surveying the room swiftly. He was clad in cutoff jeans and a plaid denim shirt and brown scuffs. His hair was too long and delightfully askew over his forehead.

She felt that trembling begin inside her again. Then the aching. The longing.

She had loved him so much. She still did.

"Like it?" he asked her, throwing his duffel bag down on the end of the elegant king-size bed.

"It's great," she said, her arms stretched out on the tub's tile rim, a small sea of bubbles around her.

He walked over to the plate glass windows to see the view of the city, now darkening with the sunset and coming to life with artificial light.

"Thanks for the dress," she told him.

He spun around. She thought again how much she liked every little thing about him, the stubborn curve of his chin, the inky color of his hair, the vivid blue of his eyes. The handsome breadth of his shoulders beneath his shirt.

He arched a brow. "Do you like it?"

She wanted to say something flippant, but only nodded.

Suddenly he started undoing the buttons of his shirt, then gave up and wrenched it over his head. He kicked off his sandals and unzipped his fly, stepped from his shorts and briefs and walked over to the tub.

She bit her lower lip, fighting the wave of hot shivers that seized her. He was entirely bronzed—except for that white streak around his hips and sex—and there wasn't a half-inch on him that could be pinched. Muscle corded his throat and shoulders and even the flatness of his belly.

She lowered her lashes quickly, wishing he didn't affect her the way he did, almost wishing she had kept her distance.

He might want her again. Wanting was easy enough.

But she wanted more. She wanted him to love her. She didn't want to be his wife because they had both forgotten to get a divorce—she wanted to be his wife because he loved her still.

As much as she loved him.

There was no way to tell him that now. Too much lay between them.

But as he sank into the water with her, an easy smile rose to her lips.

"The dress is great," she heard herself saying huskily. "Thanks. I mean, under the circumstances, I really don't have much to wear. I'll pay you back—"

"You're crew at the moment," he told her. "You don't owe me anything." He winced briefly at the heat of the water, then slid over to sit in front of one of the jets. She saw the tension ease from his face as he said, "Ah!" softly.

"Well, we'll see," she murmured.

His eyes had been closed, his head back, resting on the tiles. He opened them suddenly.

"Have you tried it on?"

"Not yet. I saw the tub and . . ."

He grinned, lacing his fingers behind his head, leaning back again. "Definitely inviting."

She nodded.

He frowned suddenly, inhaling deeply. He arched a brow at her. "What am I bathing in?" he asked.

She grinned. "Passion Flower," she told him.

He groaned.

"You don't like it?" she whispered. "Connie thought it was great. In fact, Connie told me that as crew, I could buy some and put it on your credit card."

He was silent, but his grin deepened, and his eyes were on hers. "I like it on you."

"Do you always buy bubble bath for your crew?"

"Depends on the crew member."

She started to rise, but he swiftly moved a foot, and to her surprise she found herself falling back into the slick tub.

"To the best of my knowledge, you're the only crew member for whom I've ever purchased bubble bath."

She sat still, staring at him. A moment later she felt his toes again, inching along her calf. His eyes met hers, and he smiled wolfishly.

Then she felt his toe along her inner thigh. Her upper thigh. Touching her intimately.

"Roc..." she whispered.

He grinned and came across the tub. "We've got to make love," he assured her, straddling her in the swirling water. "After all, we both smell like Passion Flower!"

She started to laugh, but then his lips sealed her laughter in her mouth, and the fullness of his body filled her with the same steaming heat that lapped around her. Her laughter was swallowed by the ecstasy that filled her, the hunger, the sweet delight. And eons later, when darkness filled the room and she lay dazed and sated and serene in the security of his arms on the expanse of the huge bed, she heard him sigh.

"I had Bruce make dinner reservations for eight. I think I'd best shower off my perfumed bubbles before we meet the gang, eh, Ms. Daven—Mrs. Trellyn?"

She felt tears sting her eyes and nodded in the darkness, hoping he didn't notice them.

He left her, striding toward the shower.

She waited a few minutes, then slipped in with him, her bar of Passion Flower in her hand while he used the soap provided by the hotel.

He looked curiously at her.

She shrugged. "Well, it worked once!" she said mischievously.

She found herself in his arms once again. "Melinda, the scent is nice. Sexy. Alluring. But you know what?"

"What?"

"You don't need a single whiff of it!"

His lips touched hers.

Why, in God's name, had they stayed apart so long?

She drew away from him, trembling again. "Dinner, eight o'clock," she reminded him.

"Eight o'clock," he agreed.

She stepped out of the shower, leaving him there. She made good use of the rest of her Passion Flower assortment, the talc and the body lotion. Then she slipped into a pair of the new silk panties, the elegant strapless dress and the sandals. When he emerged at last in a towel, she was brushing her hair and awaiting his appearance.

"Wow," he said softly.

She twirled for him. "You've always had great taste," she assured him somewhat primly.

"Yes," he said softly. "I have, haven't I?"

She started to smile as he walked over to her, then kissed her lightly. "Why don't you go on down before I get too tempted not to dress? I'll bet Connie's anxiously awaiting you by now."

"I'll wait," Melinda told him.

He groaned. "No, do me a favor, get out of here!"

She smiled, finding it very hard to leave. "All right," she told him at last. As she walked toward the door, she could feel his eyes upon her. She paused, turning back. *I love you!* she nearly cried, but she held back the words. "We'll be waiting," she told him.

She left him then, and hurried down to the Turtle Room. It was easy to find their table; the others were all there, Bruce handsome in a casual white suit, Connie lovely in a crimson flower creation, and the Tobagos a very striking couple, he in casual beige, she in striking red.

"Come, sit!" Marina called across the room to her as she entered. She hurried to their table. Bright tropical flowers adorned it. When she sat, she discovered that Connie had already ordered her the house specialty to drink. She wasn't at all sure what it was, but it was a soft orange color, and filled with pineapples and cherries and oranges. She took a sip and found it a little sweet, but good. Across the room, a calypso band was playing. The night seemed so easy, so perfect.

"Turtle steak is the specialty," Connie told her over the music.

Melinda made a face. "I've had it before. Not my favorite. I can't help feeling sorry for the turtle."

"What about cows? Have you ever seen animals with more soulful eyes?" Connie demanded.

Melinda laughed. "I don't dare think about it!" she admitted.

A moment later Roc arrived. He was wearing a light blue sport jacket and a striped shirt, no tie and darker trousers. Somehow, despite the fact that he'd packed in a duffel bag, he appeared pressed and relaxed and very handsome, his jacket emphasizing the striking color of his eyes.

He drew out the chair next to Melinda. "Have we ordered yet?"

She shook her head. "Dolphin?" she suggested.

He nodded. "The fish, of course. Not like our friend out at sea today. I learned something about him, by the way."

Her brows shot up.

"They call him Hambone. Everyone thinks he must have been in an aquarium somewhere. He's played with a number of the divers and spear fishermen around here."

"Maybe he'll stick with us!" Connie suggested.

"Maybe he's good luck," Marina said.

"Maybe," Roc agreed. Melinda felt his fingers squeeze her thigh. He reached over and sipped her drink, then made a face.

"What is it?"

"I'm not at all sure."

He grinned. Their waiter was there, and he ordered the dolphin oreganato and a beer. She ordered the dolphin, too. The rest of the table went for turtle steaks.

They talked about the dolphin, Hambone, and they talked about diving again, and Roc, his hand still resting lightly on her knee, mentioned that he was grateful for Melinda's finding the spoon, or else he would be worrying now that he was chasing a figment of his imagination.

His eyes touched hers. Cobalt. Warm.

It was a wonderful night.

They finished their food, then ordered exotic coffees. The band was playing, and people were dancing.

Roc stood at a slow number and reached down to her. She took his hand and rose swiftly, following him to the dance floor, where she leaned against his chest. His hand moved tenderly over the hair at her nape as they drifted together.

"Nice night!" he murmured.

"Very nice," she whispered against the fabric of his jacket.

Yet she had barely spoken when she suddenly felt him stiffen and go dead still.

Suddenly she realized that someone had tapped him on the shoulder.

"Excuse me, may I cut in, Trellyn? It seems you're dancing with a friend of mine!"

She instantly went cold, her hands growing clammy long before she looked up and saw Eric Longford standing at Roc's shoulder.

He was a tall man, nearly of a size with Roc, as broad shouldered, as well muscled, blond where Roc was dark, his eyes very light, his upper lip covered with a platinum mustache. Striking...

But not Roc! her heart cried out.

And then panic set in as she saw Roc's eyes. Saw him look at Eric, then felt the ice in his gaze. "Longford," he breathed very softly.

The music was still playing, but Roc wasn't holding Melinda anymore. His arms were crossed over his chest as he stared at Eric.

"Longford. Just imagine. What on earth could you be doing here?"

"Just trying to dance," Eric said, placing a hand on Melinda's shoulder.

She would have eased away—except that his was a powerful grasp.

It didn't matter.

Roc's hand suddenly fell on her other shoulder.

"Trellyn, I was cutting in—"

"But I'm not letting go," Roc said icily.

The tension was combustible. Melinda herself wanted to scream. She knew Roc, knew his thoughts.

He was thinking that Eric could only be here if she had contacted him, if she had told him where to find her. . . .

But it wasn't true!

"Trellyn, Melinda and I—"

"Longford, what's the matter? Have you lost your comprehension of the English language? You're not cutting in. Not on this dance, partner!"

Now they each had one of her hands. And each started to walk in a different direction.

So this was to be her punishment for recklessness! Drawn and quartered on the dance floor, she thought in fleeting panic.

"Eric—" she began, determined not to let this get out of hand. She had to let Roc know that she hadn't contacted anyone.

Damn him! She was furious! No matter what, he doubted her so damned quickly!

"Wait!" she tried again, jerking furiously on both hands.

But before she could go any further, she felt another set of hands fall on her shoulders. And a third male voice suddenly intervened on her behalf.

"Gentlemen! Will both of you get your hands off my daughter?"

Her father. Oh, God.

Her hands were free. She spun around. Yes, he was there. As tall, as handsome as the other men. A little older, of course, and very dignified tonight, his bronzed face ageless, his eyes so like the color of her own, his hair bleached platinum from constant exposure to the sun. His eyes held a startling twinkle.

"Dad!" she gasped.

"Oh, sure—*Dad!*" Roc said softly.

"Nice way to greet me after all this time, Trellyn," Jonathan said irritably.

"We're making a scene on the dance floor," Melinda commented wryly.

"Then dance with me," Eric suggested, taking her arm. "Let them settle old grievances!"

"Eric, if you'd just—"

"Longford, damn it!" Jonathan said firmly. "I meant what I said. Get your hands off my daughter."

"Right," Roc agreed. He took her hand again and pulled. She flew from Eric hard against Roc's tense body.

"Now, Trellyn—" Jonathan Davenport began.

"Now, nothing!" Roc nearly growled. "You can both get your hands off my *wife!*" he commanded.

Then, before anyone had a chance to say anything else, he whirled, leaving the dance floor.

And very determinedly dragging Melinda right along with him.

Chapter 10

In all his life, Roc couldn't remember being as fiercely angry as he had been when Eric Longford walked up and tapped his shoulder.

So she was there to help him! Right! And she'd just brought a few friends and close relations along for the ride!

The temptation to throw a fist into Longford's face had been overwhelming. Somehow, though, he had managed not to touch the man, despite his obvious anger.

Maybe that had had something to do with Jonathan Davenport's sudden appearance.

He couldn't deck them both.

And no matter how he itched to do so, he certainly couldn't deck Melinda.

And just when he had begun to believe . . .

"What in God's name are you doing?" she seethed at him.

What was he doing? He didn't really know. Just getting away from the entire situation as fast as possible before something did happen.

Just getting *her* away.

But as he stared into her features, pale and taut, he realized that Melinda was every bit as angry as he was. He'd dragged her from the floor, right past the dinner table, through the lobby and to the elevator.

"I've never seen anyone be so rude in my entire life!" she snapped angrily. There were people in the lobby, so she kept her voice down, but it carried a wallop of vehemence.

"Rude?" he said. *"Rude?"*

"That was my father back there—" she began.

"Oh, yeah, that's right!"

She jerked at her hand, but he had it in a vise, and he didn't let go.

"He's a salvage diver, just like you, remember? He spends a lot of time on the water, he was near here when we radioed, and Nassau is hardly a strange place to find him."

"How convenient."

She gasped suddenly, her eyes narrowing. "So I called him here, is that it? I wasn't allowed to use the radio alone, remember?"

"You could have done anything you wanted after your first day aboard. You seduced the entire crew the same way you seduced me."

She tugged hard on her hand. Too late. The elevator door had opened. He drew her through with him and punched their floor number.

He leaned against the back wall of the cubicle as it began to move, his fingers soldered to hers.

She stood very straight, outraged, indignant.

"If you think I'm going to share a room with you after the things you've been saying, you've lost your mind."

"If you think you're going back with your father or Longford, *you've* lost *your* mind."

"I didn't summon my father here. You can ask him."

The elevator reached their floor, and the door opened. Roc crossed the hallway, digging in his pocket for his key. Only when they entered the room did he release her fingers at last.

She walked farther into the room, giving herself some distance from him, and spun around. "I'm telling you—"

"Don't bother!"

He leaned against the door, staring at her, feeling a dull ache burning in his stomach, his heart. She was still crying innocent. But both Davenport and Longford were just below, and both of them had always been interested in the *Contessa.*

She admitted jumping into his net from one of Longford's boats. And tonight the tall blond man had been just itching to get his hands on her....

"I'm not staying with you," she told him quietly. She was standing very straight, her shoulders squared, her hair like spun gold tumbling around her shoulders, her eyes as bright as gems, her chin very high.

He wished the fire that was ripping through him would burn itself out. He wanted so much to take back his words. He wanted to believe her.

But he'd been burned badly before. He couldn't take any chances.

She'd done everything so smoothly. Arriving out of the blue—literally. Admitting she'd been on Longford's boat. Swimming with him—just swimming—and finding the spoon. Then continuing to search and finding nothing.

But now that she had her bearings...well, here they all were.

He shook his head, staring at her. "You have to stay here," he said flatly.

"I wouldn't stay with anyone who acted the way you have."

"Because you're so innocent. Because you're so anxious for me to lay claim to the *Contessa.*"

"Because your behavior is horrible."

He was still leaning against the door. It seemed to be giving him strength. "You said that you'd stay here," he reminded her.

"I'm not going to my father or—or anyone!" she snapped to him impatiently. "I simply can't stay with you after everything you've accused me of doing!"

He swept his arm out, indicating the still tousled bed where they had found a few precious moments of abandon.

"It's yours," he told her. "I've slept on numerous floors. I'll just take the bedspread and a pillow."

"I don't think you understand!" she exclaimed. "I don't want to be near anyone who's convinced that I'm such a horrible human being!"

"And I don't think you understand. You're not leaving."

She whirled around, heading for the glass windows to stare out at the city below. "All right, Captain Trellyn!" she snapped, her voice as cold as dripping icicles. "Fine. I won't leave this room. I'll finish the entire search without saying a word to another living soul. But you just keep your distance from me, do you understand?"

Keep his distance from her...

When he already hated what he had started, when he was ready to give up the whole damned hunt just to have her again, with no need to hold her, because she would stay of her own free will, just to be with him.

He felt ill, but stood straight, feeling very cold himself. So distant. That was what she wanted.

The phone rang suddenly, jarringly. Melinda jumped, then stared at it without moving.

It kept ringing.

"I'm certainly not going to answer it and give away the great secrets of the deep!" she exclaimed.

"Why not? It's your father—or your *dear friend* Longford."

She didn't move, so he crossed the room and yanked the receiver off the phone. "What?"

" 'Hello' is the more customary response," Jonathan Davenport informed him lightly.

" 'What do you want?' is far more appropriate under the circumstances. Although I'm assuming I know what you want. To speak with your daughter. Well, I'm sorry. She can't talk tonight."

Melinda was staring at him with a fury that promised to be explosive. Then he forgot about her, suddenly startled by Jonathan's response. "Can't talk to her, eh? Is she bound and gagged? Never mind, that wouldn't be your style. I just wanted to make sure she was all right."

"She's absolutely wonderful—for a woman wearing a gag."

"Why don't you meet me for a drink?" Jonathan suggested.

"Why?"

"Maybe you'd be willing to give me a chance to talk to you. Maybe you'd even be willing to give me a chance to apologize."

Roc kept staring at Melinda, stunned. Old man Davenport wanting to apologize?

It could be true. Maybe somewhere along the line he had decided that he had been wrong. Maybe he'd even told his daughter that he'd been wrong.

"Yeah," he said slowly. Melinda was stil staring at him.

"There's a small bar off the main lobby. I'll be there," Davenport told him.

Roc replaced the receiver, still staring at Melinda. He lifted a hand to indicate the room. "It's all yours."

"What are you doing?" she demanded, suddenly running after him as he headed for the door. Her eyes were suddenly anxious, the chill gone from her voice.

"Well, I'm not going out to get into a brawl with your father. Is that what you're worried about?"

She fell silent, staring at him.

"I won't be gone long," he said swiftly.

He turned and exited the room with long strides, then leaned against the door once he had closed it behind him. He waited for a long moment, wondering if she would follow.

But she didn't.

He found the bar easily enough, and Jonathan Davenport more easily. He was sitting on one of the bar stools—with Connie by his side.

They made a startlingly attractive couple, both slim and blond, both tanned. Jonathan, of course, despite the fact that he looked damned good for his age, was still a more mature individual, with his bronzed face and craggy features. But Connie was laughing delightedly at something he was saying, glowing, her velvet brown eyes wide and bright. She was very pretty in the crimson dress that enhanced her pale hair and darker eyes. And Jonathan *was* a handsome man.

Perhaps he needed to have been, to have something to do with the creation of his daughter.

Despite the age difference—at least sixteen or seventeen years—the two looked good together.

Then Roc scowled suddenly, wondering just what Connie was doing with the man. Where the hell was Bruce?

Bruce was her brother, not her keeper, he reminded himself, admitting that his mood was raw, his temper still frayed. Only curiosity had brought him here. At least Melinda couldn't go running out to talk to her father, since he would be talking to Jonathan himself.

Which left Eric Longford, of course.

And that called for a Scotch.

He walked across the crowded bar and slid into the seat on the other side of Jonathan.

Connie's brown eyes went very wide. ''Roc! I was just—I guess the two of you want to talk. I think I'll take a walk through the lobby.''

She leaped up, disappearing before either of them could protest.

Roc ordered a drink swiftly, then sipped it, staring at his old friend and mentor. He looked good. And clean living, Roc decided, hadn't done it.

''Sweet girl,'' Jonathan said lightly, referring to Connie.

''Little young for you,'' Roc commented.

Jonathan shrugged. "Maybe. But I always thought interests and compatibility were more important than age."

Roc lifted his glass to Jonathan. "That's because you're aging," he informed him.

Jonathan laughed, not offended in the least. He ran his fingers up and down his beer glass, staring at the amber liquid. "So she's bound and gagged, eh?"

"You don't want to run up and rescue your daughter?" Roc said.

Jonathan shrugged, turning to stare at Roc at last, his eyes so like his daughter's, determined. "That depends," he said.

"On what?"

"Is it true that my daughter is still your wife?" Jonathan demanded.

It was Roc's turn to shrug. "Well, Davenport, I never divorced her. So if she never filed papers against me, then she's still my wife."

Jonathan nodded. "Well, then . . ." he murmured.

"Well, then what?"

"Well, then—I'm not going to go up and rescue her. This is between the two of you."

Roc took a sip of his Scotch. "She was on one of Longford's boats when she dived into my net, you know."

Davenport seemed to wince. "She does have that reckless streak in her."

"She wasn't with you," Roc commented.

"Of course she wasn't!" Davenport replied indignantly. "I would never have let her pull such a stunt, and she would have damned well known it. She must have wheedled Longford—" He broke off, maybe realizing instinctively just how Roc felt about the other man. He shrugged again. "Well, she hadn't been with him long. We were in Miami together the morning before you called me, so they had just gone out on a day trip."

"I'll give you this, Jonathan, you do make more of an effort to explain her behavior than she does."

"Well, she didn't really know she had to explain her behavior, did she now? You two have been apart for a long time."

"It was her choice," Roc reminded him.

Jonathan nodded, his eyes downcast for a moment. "Her choice and my mistake then," he said, staring at Roc again. "I was wrong—the find was yours. Even if the salvage should have been shared, the credit should have been yours. Maybe I was just so damned irritated that you could be so right—and against all the odds I quoted you. Maybe I just couldn't believe that I could be so wrong. It's late. Too damned late for me, really, but not for Melinda. . . ."

Roc felt his heart thundering. "What do you mean?"

"Well, you said it was her choice back then. It's her choice now, too, isn't it? And she wound up on your boat, right?"

"Coming from Longford's," he reminded Jonathan.

"Maybe you should think about this, then. Longford was always attracted to her, and she never wanted to give him the time of day. She was always polite, and I won't lie to you, we've been thrown together enough over the past few years. She's still polite. A friend. That's it."

"Why are you telling me all this?"

"Because my daughter's bound and gagged up in your room," Jonathan said cheerfully.

Roc sat back, feeling a smile curve his lips, feeling as if the warmth of his Scotch had spread through his whole body, searing away the cold.

"She was in a rather bad position, you know," Jonathan said suddenly.

"Pardon?"

"Well, you put her in a rough position—a choice between her closest blood relative and the man she loved."

"She went for the relative," Roc said lightly.

"Well, there was a time when I was all she had. And, admittedly, I did do my best to sway her at the time."

"And now?" Roc asked.

"And now, well..." His voice trailed away; then he finished his beer and looked at Roc again. "Well, now I was just relieved to discover that she was on board with *you* and not Longford."

"So you'd be swaying her in my direction?"

Jonathan shook his head. "I've learned my lesson the hard way. I wouldn't sway anyone in any direction."

"Then—"

"She was in your damned boat, and she's in your room now, right?" Jonathan demanded.

"Bound and gagged," Roc reminded him.

Jonathan smiled. "I just wanted to let you know that a pigheaded treasure seeker was wrong once, and that I'm sorry. And that I hope you do find your *Contessa.* Although I hear you're well under way."

"She did get in touch with you, then—" Roc began.

"No." Davenport shook his head. He indicated the now empty seat at his side. "Your crew member was telling me that my daughter brought up a spoon from the ship."

Connie. Hmm.

"Yeah, Melinda brought up a spoon."

"She's a good diver. The best. Treasure what you've got."

Roc stood. Three years had been a long time. Davenport had changed. So had Melinda. And so had he.

"Thanks for calling," Roc said, setting a hand on Davenport's back.

Davenport grinned and nodded. "The best of luck."

"With the treasure? Or your daughter?"

"If you haven't seen yet that she's the real treasure, then you're searching in the dark, my boy."

Roc laughed. "I'll take that to heart, Jonathan. Good night."

He left the bar behind, anxious to return to his room. To the beautiful view, the clean white sheets, the cool air...

His wife.

If she forgave him. He'd been seeing only the awful vision of himself on the floor—the great whirlpool empty, the bed a haven of nothing more than ice for him.

At least they'd had a little time together before...

Before he'd acted like a Neanderthal, he admitted to himself, striding toward the elevator.

She might still be angry. Unwilling to forgive him.

But then, apologies weren't so hard. He'd just learned that from his father-in-law.

There was a sudden tapping on his shoulder, and he spun around. All the warmth that had been flooding him abruptly turned glacial.

Eric Longford. Very tall, beach-boy blond. Face knotted in an ugly grimace.

"You've got a lot of nerve, Trellyn!" he grated furiously.

"I've got nothing to say to you, Longford," Roc began. Then he saw that Melinda was not waiting for him upstairs. She was standing just behind Longford.

His heart sank anew, and his temper flared.

"Take a hike, Longford," he said, and started to turn. Melinda could go wherever she damn well pleased. He started toward the elevator.

"Not on your life, Trellyn!"

The hand hit his shoulder again, spinning him around. He tensed and ducked just in time to miss Eric's flying right fist.

"Damn it, Longford," he snapped, but Eric was swinging again.

That was the end of the line for Roc. He ducked and came up with a fast right hook himself, catching Eric right beneath the chin.

The big blond fell cleanly backward, out cold.

"Roc!"

It was Melinda, furious, falling to her knees by Longford's side. "Roc, this is no way—"

"Let's go," he told her, reaching down and catching her hand.

He dragged her to her feet. A crowd was milling, but luckily, most of the assembled people had seen Eric taking the first swing.

Someone else could pick up his nemesis. Melinda damn well wasn't going to do it.

He strode into the elevator with her. They were alone. The door closed.

Melinda spun on him. "You didn't need to knock him out! Hitting a man never solved anything—"

"He swung at me."

"You—"

"Twice! And you—what the hell were you doing downstairs with him?"

"What? Oh, all right, you idiot. I was down there trying to give him the most exact directions I could on right where I found the spoon!"

"Were you?"

She took a wild swing at him, but he caught her, holding her tightly in his arms. "Anyone would try to hit you!" she cried out furiously.

"What were you doing?"

"I wasn't even with him!" she cried out, struggling in his arms.

The elevator door opened. He kept a firm hand on her while he fumbled for his key, found it, then ushered them both through the door.

He leaned against it again. "So, what were you doing downstairs?"

"I don't owe you an explanation. Your behavior just keeps getting worse and worse!"

He crossed the room toward her, and she tried to back away. "You keep your distance from me. I mean it!"

But he came closer, and she backed around the big whirlpool tub.

"You have no right!"

"I'm just asking!" he told her, coming relentlessly closer. He had to touch her again. They just couldn't waste such a great room. . . .

"And I—" she began.

He caught her upper arms and pulled her against him. "What?" he asked.

"Connie called up and told me you were in the bar with my father!" she cried furiously. "I came down to make sure you were both all right!"

Tears glazed her eyes. Suddenly his mouth ground down on hers as his long strides brought them to the bed. Together they fell to the mattress, and it seemed as if they sank into an embrace of softness.

Her hands pressed against his chest. "Roc, you can't do this to me. It's not fair. It's not right. It's—"

"I'm sorry," he said softly.

"What?" Her eyes were very wide, so beautiful with their damp glaze.

How had he lived without her for so long?

He kissed her lips lightly. Caught her hand and brought it to his lips and kissed her fingers. "I'm sorry," he told her.

"But you'll be suspicious again—"

"I'll try not to be. Melinda, you just suddenly appeared back in my life when I'd nearly managed to get over you. My manners aren't great, and I might act like a bastard again."

"Then sorry isn't enough!" she charged.

"Melinda, damn it, I love you!" he cried. "Isn't that enough?"

She was silent. Not breathing. Then she whispered. "Oh, my lord..."

"Well?"

Her arms wound around his neck. Her lips touched his. Her tongue circled them, then dove into his mouth. She kissed him heatedly, passionately.

But he broke away from her, staring down at her. "Well?"

"It's enough!" she cried. "It's enough!"

His lips found hers once again.

And later, much later, she whispered softly to him, "Roc?"

"Yes?"

"I..."

"Yes?"

She rose above him, hair wild, eyes dazzling, her naked flesh warm to his touch.

"I love you," she told him. "I never stopped loving you. I tried, I tried so hard, but..."

His arm slid round her, and he swept her down beside him, then kissed her forehead.

Davenport was right. He would keep looking for the *Contessa,* of course. But he already held treasure in his arms. It was just a matter of keeping her now.

Chapter 11

"All right, get ready now. . . ."

Melinda looked at Roc, ten feet to her left, then at Joe, ten feet to her right. Connie was another ten feet to Joe's right, and then Bruce was about ten feet away from his sister, and they were all treading water, waiting for Marina to give them the go sign.

"We're ready!" Roc called out, exasperated.

"Eh!" Marina cried, lifting her chin. "I am the starter here. Now, you men, mind you! The first one to touch the boat is the one who wins, eh?"

"We've got it, Marina!" Bruce called. "But we're all going to turn into prunes out here if we don't—"

"Go!" Marina cried.

Bruce, of course, was left to gasp in a breath before he could shoot through the water with his first stroke, already giving the others an advantage.

Melinda knew she was fast, but she wasn't quite as fast as Roc. She started out just a hair ahead of him, and she swam for all she was worth. She knew she was well past Connie and Bruce—she was even level with Joe Tobago—but just as she neared the boat—right when she was nearly touching it!—Roc pulled ahead strongly, beating her.

Gasping for breath, he held on to the ladder to the bow, shaking a raised fist in the air and letting out something like a victory cry. Melinda clung to the other side of the ladder.

"Beat you!" he told her.

She shrugged, grinning.

"Right! You beat your ninety-pound wife!" Marina chastised from above them.

"Oh, Marina, she's way more than ninety pounds!" Roc said, crawling out of the water.

"Hey!" Melinda protested.

"All right, maybe not *way* more." He leaped into the boat, offered her a hand and helped her aboard.

Joe crawled up behind her. "Ah, well, the lady has put me to shame!" he said, shaking his head and grinning.

Melinda smiled and reminded him, "But I didn't dive today, and you did." It was their first day back over the old World War Two wreck since they had left Nassau. They hadn't gotten out nearly as early in the morning after their night's stay as Roc had intended—partially because neither he nor Melinda woke until nearly noon, and then, since no one had bothered to inform them about the time, they proceeded to squander a lot more of it.

It had been nice squandering, Melinda thought.

But once they were up, Roc still had to see that provisions were brought aboard. There were lists to check and double-check, and it was dusk when they finally managed to leave Nassau Harbor behind.

This morning she'd been tired. But it didn't matter. For the moment she was content to merely cherish this time. She didn't know what her father had said to Roc—she hadn't had a chance to see Jonathan again. She was certain, of course, that her father felt just fine about the way events were occurring, though. If he hadn't, he would have been tearing down hotel walls. He and Roc were an awful lot alike when it came to their protective, macho habits.

She hadn't really said much more to Roc about the past, either. Maybe he still didn't trust her completely.

Or her father.

But though she thought it was understandable that she had taken her father's side on that long ago occasion, she had to admit that she had done so instantly and completely—she had never given Roc a chance at all. Maybe it took time to come back from something like that, although it seemed that at least they now had time on their hands.

He was still after the *Contessa.* Naturally. But he seemed to have slowed down just a little bit in his pursuit. They seemed to dally longer over breakfast, lunch, dinner. They stayed out on deck, staring up at the stars. They still woke with the dawn, but they didn't quite manage to rise with it, and the whole of the *Crystal Lee* seemed to be more relaxed.

Maybe there was still a barrier between them, though. Roc didn't talk about the future. No matter how close they were becoming, he was keeping a certain distance.

She might still be his wife. And she might be sharing his life, his bed and now, his work. But she didn't know what would happen when they found the *Contessa*—or failed in their attempt.

"Hey! How about a hand here?" Connie called, climbing up the ladder.

Roc quickly responded, then helped Bruce aboard behind her.

"I think we need a rematch!" Bruce complained.

"I think I had better start supper," Marina said.

"I think," Peter called from the helm, where he had been surveying the nearby waters with binoculars, "that it's time for a beer!"

Melinda grinned at him, then noticed that, despite the lightness of his voice, something seemed to be bothering him.

He came down a second later and joined the rest of them as they tramped into the galley, popping soda and beer cans, pretending to help Marina but really getting in her way.

"Melinda," Marina called to her. "Do you mind slicing some fresh vegetables?"

"Just tell me what you want sliced and diced," she said cheerfully. "Other than the captain, of course," she added sweetly.

Roc offered her a warning frown, which she ignored, but as she sliced a carrot, she looked out the window and saw that he was standing beside Peter, staring out into the coming night with the binoculars.

Darkness seemed to fall swiftly that night. The sun had been setting while they'd been in the water, and then boom—it was dark. Melinda squinted, trying to see through the galley portholes. There seemed to be a light out on the water.

She arranged the vegetables on the platter Marina had indicated, left Connie and Bruce setting the table and Joe Tobago marking one of the maps they were using for their dives.

Marina looked at her as she started out, and Melinda promised to be right back.

"Everything is nearly ready," Marina assured her. "Take your time."

Melinda nodded and went out on the deck, shivering a little as she came up behind Peter and Roc. She hadn't had a chance to shower and change yet, and the night air had quickly become chilly.

They were murmuring together, but they fell silent, turning as she reached them.

Roc's jaw was tight, a sure sign that though his words might not give him away, something wasn't to his liking.

"What is it?" she asked.

"Another boat," he told her.

She didn't like the sound of his voice. It had an edge to it. She felt a chill sweep over her, and she was instantly defensive.

He had no right to keep doing this to her.

"How amazing," she said coolly. "These are temperate, beautiful waters! Why on earth would anyone want to sail around here?"

Her sarcasm wasn't lost on Roc, who cast her a quick, warning glare.

"Well," Peter said, "she's keeping her distance now. Nothing more than a dot on the horizon for the night. We'll see what she does in the morning, eh, *mi amigo?*"

"Si," Roc agreed. He had been in South Florida and among the islands constantly enough over the years to pick up both Spanish and island French. Then he said something else to Peter in Spanish—which Melinda didn't understand. He hadn't meant for her to understand, she realized angrily.

She gritted her teeth. She had been on the boat alone today for a while. Even Marina had joined the divers since Hambone, their dolphin friend, had made another appearance.

So here she was. Guilty again. No matter what. Roc was obviously thinking that she had climbed to the radio in her first moment alone. And summoned . . . ?

Someone. Her father. Eric.

She swung around, having nothing else to say to either of them, though the sympathetic glance Peter had given her seemed to tell her that he was on her side.

Well, she didn't need anyone on her side. Because she wasn't guilty.

She started walking down the deck. "Melinda!" Roc called to her sharply. "I'd like a word with you."

"Later," she said coolly. "If you don't mind. I'm freezing, and I think I'll shower quickly before dinner."

She marched into the cabin, rummaged through one of Roc's bottom drawers for the strange clothing collection she was acquiring, grabbed a towel and stepped into the tiny shower.

She was grateful for the blast of hot water. She lifted her face to it, then nearly screamed aloud as the shower curtain came crashing open.

He was there, of course, cobalt eyes narrowed, hard.

"What was that all about?" he asked her.

She reached for the shower curtain, trying to wrench it back. His fingers remained tightly around it. "Do you mind?" she inquired tightly.

"I do," he assured her. "Why did you stomp off like that?"

"There's a boat out there. Of course I must have summoned it, right?"

"There's a boat out there. And I think it's your father's."

She gasped aloud, then tugged harder on the curtain. "You've spoken to my father since I have!" she said angrily. "Remember? I couldn't be trusted to talk to him!"

"But you two are very close," he reminded her.

She swore at him as he stepped into the shower with her, still clad only in his swimming trunks.

"Don't do this to me!" she charged him. "Roc, I'm warning you—"

The water splattered both their faces as he drew her into his arms, then took her lips with a very wet, hot kiss. His hands slid erotically over her body along with the water, cupping her buttocks, drawing her close to his half naked body.

She broke away from his lips, feeling the pounding of the water between them. "You don't accuse someone one moment—"

"I haven't accused you at all," he told her huskily. She heard a splatting sound and realized that he had dropped his trunks to the floor and she was suddenly in his arms again.

"You just said—"

"I said I think it might be your father's boat!" he told her firmly, cobalt eyes fiercely on hers.

"Because—"

"Because he's out there!" he exclaimed, aggravated. The water was still deliciously warm, cascading over them. He leaned her back against the wall, his kiss openmouthed, demanding. Both his touch and the falling water were instantly arousing, and she found herself breathless, still trying to argue, but forgetting what she was arguing about.

Suddenly his hands were on her hips and he was lifting her, then bringing her swiftly down on his sex, urging her to wrap her legs around him. Dizzy with the sweet sensations, she obeyed instantly, her arms wrapping around him as well, fingers digging into the wet thickness of his hair, then grasping his shoulders. A soft moan escaped her as he thrust swift and hard within her, again and again. He very quickly drove her wild, his speed and movement suddenly a tempest, one that burst upon her in a sweet, sudden, shattering moment.

Then she felt him easing her down against the length of him. She felt the water beating against her face and breast again. Her knees were steady, but that didn't matter; he lifted her out of the shower, wrapping her in a towel and holding her tenderly.

A moment later he glanced at his watch. "Damn," he murmured softly.

Her face had been burrowed against his chest. Now she looked up. Teasing eyes touched her own.

"I think we've missed dinner."

She grabbed his wrist, staring at his watch, and groaned, unable to believe that she had walked out of the galley to find him on the deck nearly a full hour ago.

"You seem to have a thing for making me miss meals," she told him.

"Pardon?"

"You did drag me away from my dolphin oreganato in Nassau," she reminded him, toweling dry quickly and trying to step around him.

"We weren't eating, we were dancing then, remember? And you were about to dance off with Longford."

She gritted her teeth. "I wasn't about to dance off with anyone." She walked past him to dress in the cabin.

He followed her out, but he didn't bother to dress, just stretched out naked on the bunk, watching her.

"I wonder why the hell he was there," Roc mused.

Her eyes quickly shot to him. "I'm telling you—"

"I didn't accuse you!"

"But every time something happens, you have one hell of a way of looking at me!"

"I like looking at you," he assured her.

She pulled on a long sleeved T-shirt over a pair of jeans. "Would you come on now, please? What is your crew going to think when we both disappear—"

"Oh," Roc said offhandedly, "they're probably going to think that we're having sex in my cabin."

"Roc, damn you!"

He started to laugh, leaping up. He set his hands on her shoulders and kissed her lips lightly. "I'll be right along," he assured her.

She nodded. But for some reason, she didn't like the look in his eyes at all.

No matter what his words were, the barriers remained.

And she had already risked so much of her heart again. She shivered suddenly, thinking that this had become so much more dangerous than it had seemed at the beginning.

After all, she had merely jumped into the sea and waited to be dragged up in a fishing net.

While now...

Now the stakes were very high indeed. Much, much higher than the riches of the *Contessa*.

She awoke ahead of Roc the next morning and dressed quickly. Finding herself the first one up, she started coffee and breakfast. She was already sipping coffee, the bacon was nearly crisp, and she'd managed a huge pile of scrambled eggs with peppers and mushrooms, when Marina came yawning into the galley, smiling delightedly, saying she would be happy to take over.

"Wake the captain gently with coffee!" Marina suggested, and Melinda grinned, then started to leave the galley.

"Melinda!" Marina said, calling her back suddenly.

She paused, curious, and turned. Marina was studying her gravely. "You're a real asset on board," Marina told her.

Melinda smiled. From Marina, it was quite a compliment.

"Thanks," she said softly.

She left the galley, bringing coffee to the captain's cabin for Roc. As she entered and closed the door behind her, she remembered how miserably jealous she had been of Connie. That hadn't been so long ago. Now Connie was proving to be a good friend.

And she was bringing Roc his coffee. Even if suspicion still lurked in those cobalt eyes . . .

She found him awake, leaning comfortably on a pillow, the covers pulled to his waist. He smiled, just like a king, and she knew he had been waiting patiently and serenely for his coffee to arrive.

"Thanks," he said, reaching for the cup and pulling her down to sit by his side. "I like having a wife aboard. Coffee in bed. Sheer luxury."

"It wasn't so bad before," Melinda reminded him primly. "Connie brought you your coffee."

"But not in bed."

Melinda shrugged. "I think she would have if you had wanted her to."

"Maybe."

"I ought to pour this all over you!"

He laughed and offered her a sip. She took it. "You're a jealous little thing," he told her.

"Neither jealous nor little, remember?" she told him.

"Little to me, and I think that a little bit of jealousy is great."

"Feeds the ego, huh?"

He nodded gravely. "Your ego must be pretty nicely inflated, then."

She frowned.

There was more tension in his voice than she would have liked. "Longford! I really enjoyed decking that guy." He reached out and touched her hair suddenly. "I think that if he had ever touched you..."

"What?" she asked.

He shook his head. The look in his eyes made her feel warm. Nicely warm.

"Breakfast is nearly on. You need to get up."

"I am up," he said innocently.

She leaped away from the bed, laughing. "I really can't afford to miss any more meals or I *will* be a little thing!" she warned him.

"I'll be right along," he promised her, throwing the covers aside. She was very careful to keep her eyes on his. "Are you diving with me this morning?" he asked her.

"Yes."

"Good."

An hour and a half later, they were ready to start.

Peter was at the helm with his binoculars, but there wasn't another vessel of any kind in view this morning. It seemed that they were alone with the endless blue sky and sea, without even a cloud on the horizon.

Bruce and Connie went over the edge first, paired up for their dive. Melinda and Roc followed in a few minutes, entering the strange, exotic world that so fascinated them both.

They swam down to the ledge directly over the old wreck. Tangs and clown fish darted by, and a jellyfish floated eerily a distance away.

Something bright in the sand attracted Roc's attention, and he swam down to it, listening to the familiar sounds of his regulator and air bubbles. He felt a rush of water and turned in time to see Hambone making a dive behind him. He watched the dolphin, then turned his attention to the sand. He shot deeper, digging around one of the rusted masts from the World War Two ship.

Hambone dove by him again. A second later he looked just past the mast to see that Melinda was playing with the dolphin, stroking him, catching on to his flipper, taking a swim with him.

He looked toward the mast again, then dug around it some more. Nothing. He didn't know what he had seen.

He looked for Melinda again and saw her diving past a section of the bow of the ship. She disappeared, following the dolphin once again, so it seemed.

He sighed inwardly. He didn't like her disappearing. He quickly swam in her direction, his flippers shooting him swiftly through the water.

There she was, making a startling beeline to him already. He paused, ready for a collision with her, but the force of the water just brought her right to him, where she began trying to talk around her mouthpiece, letting out strange sounds in the aquamarine depths.

Then she lifted her hands. She was holding a small chest, so covered in soft green growth that it was amazing she had seen the thing. It was just the size of a lady's jewel box. Maybe a lady from a very different time...

He nodded to her, and they kicked the water, rising swiftly to the surface. He called out, and Joe was quickly there to help them from the water. He took the prize out of Melinda's hands while she climbed aboard, stripping off her equipment.

"Roc! It's something, isn't it?"

"Something? Of course," he agreed, taking the piece. It was eight inches along, he thought, four deep, four wide. The top was arched. He tapped on it gently and looked at Melinda.

"Brass, I think."

He turned and started down to the equipment room, finding a tiny wedge to set in the indentation he at last discovered in the chest.

Melinda was behind him, along with Marina and Joe. Peter was out on deck yelling to Bruce and Connie, who had just surfaced, to hurry in.

The chest popped open.

There was no dank green growth inside. The brilliance of the gems was startling. The small container was filled to overflowing with necklaces, earrings, brooches, pins.

"My God!" Melinda breathed.

Roc's eyes touched hers. "Quite a find!" he exclaimed softly. He shook his head. "How on earth do you do it?"

"How do you find the right stretch of ocean floor?" she asked him in return.

"I've got to match this with the *Contessa*'s manifest," he told her, "but I'm sure we've really made an incredible find."

"Then we stake our claim—"

"I want a better idea of where she's really lying, first," he said softly. "But this is the main step. We should be ready in another day or two."

"Hey, how's it going down there?" Bruce called down.

"We're coming up. Wait until you see this!" Roc replied.

They started up the stairs to the main deck. Suddenly they saw Peter's face right above them.

"And you," he warned softly, his voice tense, "should see what else we've discovered up here."

Roc looked at Melinda.

She felt that awful, awful cold again.

"What?" he asked Peter. "Another boat?"

"Not another boat," Peter said. "*Two* boats. And moving in very, very quickly!"

Chapter 12

There were definitely two boats very near them, one to the south, one to the north.

As Roc stood by the rail of the *Crystal Lee,* Peter handed him the binoculars, and he stared out.

Melinda saw him stiffen as he looked north, then seemed to harden to concrete as he looked to the south.

She didn't need binoculars to recognize either boat. It was her father's newest to their north. And it was Eric Longford's well-equipped search vessel to the south.

She was damned. He didn't have to open his mouth. She was already damned.

"Company," Peter said lightly.

"It doesn't matter anymore," Bruce said, standing close by Roc's shoulder. "We've got the spoon, and the casket. It's time to go ashore, fill out the papers and pull out the heavy equipment ourselves."

Roc lowered the glasses and pointed across the water. "They're already diving from Longford's boat," he commented. "And we still don't have a fix on the damned position of the *Contessa.* You know, it is amazing—*amazing!*—that after all these weeks, Davenport and Longford home in so exactly on our location."

He wasn't looking at Melinda. He didn't need to look at her. There was an edge in his voice, cold, sarcastic.

For a fleeting moment she wondered just what in hell her father was trying to do to her. Then she felt a shivering deep inside. It seemed to start at the base of her tailbone, then send icy little fingers to curl around her heart.

She couldn't change things. She couldn't go back. Something had broken between them years ago, and now his barrier against her was always in place. He would condemn her at the drop of a hat.

She couldn't change it, and she couldn't live with it.

She turned away from the group. She had on her black one-piece bathing suit—exactly what she had arrived in. She wasn't going to fight with Roc anymore. And she couldn't plead with him anymore to believe in her. Maybe it was time to go.

"We're being radioed!" Connie called suddenly, hurrying up to the helm, Roc close behind her. Standing in the cool breeze below, Melinda couldn't hear their conversation. But a second later Roc came down, his face thunderous, eyes furiously dark and flashing. He didn't say anything at first, just stood by the rail, looking at Longford's boat.

Then he spun around, staring at Melinda. "It was for you," he told her very politely. "He says that he's here now, and has suggested that you might want to swim back."

Melinda felt the blood draining from her face, but kept her chin high. She shook her head. "I never—"

"Then there's your father, of course. Only one of them had to know where we are. The other one simply followed! Maybe you didn't call Longford. Maybe you just called dear old Dad."

"Roc!" Connie gasped.

"Roc, maybe—" Peter began.

"This is between us!" Roc snapped, staring at Melinda. "Damn it, don't you think I've wanted to believe all along? My God, she snapped her fingers and I was back like a puppy on a string. In all the seven seas, she's the only damn thing ever to undo me!"

He was clearly angry, but there was something else in his voice, too. Maybe an edge of anguish. But it didn't matter. He couldn't hurt the way she was hurting; he couldn't feel as if a knife had been thrust right down his gullet. Maybe she hadn't earned his total trust, but she didn't deserve this.

His eyes, burning ice, ripped into her. "Well?" he said, and suddenly his voice was soft.

Well. This was it.

"Don't you have anything to say?" he suggested.

She walked the few feet across to him, her heart seeming to shatter into little pieces as she did so. She stopped right in front of him and met his gaze. "No!" she said flatly.

"Lord," he whispered softly. "So you admit—"

She'd meant to leave with a little bit of dignity, but this was the wrong side of too much.

She swung at him without thought, her hand cracking against his chin. The sound was loud, and her palm was left stinging.

This time, she thought fleetingly, they had quite an audience for the death of their relationship. Now they would all know that she really was the Iron Maiden, the witch of the sea.

It couldn't be helped.

Neither could the tears that were stinging her eyes like acid.

Roc didn't respond to her slap other than to raise his fingers to his reddening flesh, though she couldn't really see his face; she couldn't see at all anymore.

She did know which way was north. She turned and headed down the port side rail, leaped up, then plunged into the sea.

She dived deep and swam a good distance beneath the water before surfacing. When she did, she heard him shouting to her.

"Oh, no, you don't! Get back here!"

She looked. He was poised on the rail, then leaping in after her.

She looked at her father's boat. It seemed to have moved farther away since she had entered the water.

She started to swim. She had a head start, and she was nearly as fast as Roc.

She swam hard, streaking through the water. Yet almost impossibly, two seconds later, Roc had reached her, his arm winding around her middle, sending the two of them plummeting into the depths.

He let go of her then, and she shot to the surface. He rose alongside her. She stared at him in disbelief, and then she saw the dolphin's fin.

Hambone. Hambone had come along just in time to give Roc a nice ride. And now that he had caught up with her, the same ice-hard look was in his eyes. "Back!" he told her.

"For what?"

"To finish this thing."

She shook her head, the tears stinging her eyes fiercely once again. "It *is* finished. It was finished three years ago. I was just too stupid to realize how final it was. I—"

"Back!" he insisted again.

"I'm not giving you any explanations—"

"You're not going to your father or Longford—"

"I *am* going to my father!" she cried. She turned, stroking determinedly through the water once again.

A hand clenched on her ankle, and she found herself jerked back.

The amount of struggling she was doing would have drowned anyone else, she thought, but not Roc. He'd managed to get a hold on her, and no matter how she twisted and flailed, there was only so much damage she could do. Gasping, choking, furious—but spent—she finally went limp in his hold. She didn't think she'd ever been so miserable in her life, feeling his touch, the power of his hands, and knowing that he wouldn't listen to her, didn't believe in her, and that somehow, though she still loved him despite her fury, she was going to have to escape him.

He reached the ladder at the bow of the *Crystal Lee*. She had very little choice except to climb ahead of him. Connie was there, her pretty face troubled, ready to offer a towel. Roc came up right behind Melinda; she felt him at her back. His hand fell on her shoulder, and she whirled. "Don't you touch me! Don't touch me, and don't speak to me! I've done all the pleading I can do with you. I've—"

"There are two boats right out there!" he roared.

She started to walk past him, but he grabbed her arm and swung her around until both his hands were clutching her upper arms in a relentless hold. "Tell me how the hell they got here!"

There was something desperate in his words, in his hold. He held her in a vice, but his hands and fingers shook with emotion.

"Go to hell!" she cried back.

"Stop!" Connie shrieked suddenly. She ran to the two of them, then stopped, biting her lower lip, her eyes miserable. "I did it!" she said. "Roc—I did it!"

"Oh, Connie! Don't!" Melinda whispered.

"Connie—" Roc began.

"You don't understand!" she said swiftly. She looked quickly from one to the other of them. She shook her head, looking into Roc's eyes. "I spent a lot of time with Jonathan Davenport the other night. In the bar, when you came in. And then later..." Her voice trailed away. Melinda felt her eyes widen. Connie? And her *father?* "Roc, if he's doing anything, he's trying to help you. He doesn't want the *Contessa,* he just wants to see that everything goes smoothly for you. And naturally he was worried about his daughter. He's just here to help. I'm sure of it! I'm sorry, Roc, I didn't mean to cause any trouble."

Roc shook his head, his hold on Melinda easing. "It's all right, Connie. We've both been seduced."

"Ahoy there!"

They all swung around, staring toward the bow, where Jonathan Davenport was now securing his dinghy, then reaching for the ladder. He was in cutoffs, bare-chested and barefooted, light hair in disarray over his forehead, aquamarine eyes very bright.

Melinda frowned at her father, then realized that he was a striking man and only in his mid-forties. Maybe he was just right for Connie, and Connie for him.

If any of them could survive the next few moments...

Jonathan stared across the bow to where Roc was standing with Melinda. "She almost had you that time," he informed Roc matter-of-factly. "Am I losing my mind, or did you get a little help from a dolphin there?"

"I had a little help," Roc said.

"How's it going, kitten?" Jonathan asked his daughter softly.

"Kitten!" Roc snorted. He met her eyes. "Barracuda!" he assured her.

She kicked his shin. He winced, but offered no retaliation.

"Hi, Dad!" she murmured to her father. He could be off on his own, but he was standing here, just about doing somersaults to help her. She felt an overwhelming tenderness for him and wanted to hug him fiercely.

"Well," Jonathan said matter-of-factly, "I really wouldn't want to break up whatever it is that's going on here, but I think you should know that Eric has divers down below. Don't you have anything on which to base a claim?" he asked Roc.

Roc's hands eased from Melinda's shoulders. "Melinda has found a few things," he said. "But I still don't have a fix on the ship itself."

"Radar isn't yielding—" Jonathan began.

"Radar gives us a World War Two wreck," Roc said.

"Well, I've got a suggestion for you," Jonathan said. "I'll take Melinda back to my boat with me, along with another diver or two. Let me get back, looking as if I've just come to rescue my daughter from your clutches, then you hightail it into shore to make your claim. Melinda can go down and keep up the hunt. If you've come this close, it has to be right under your nose."

"I don't think Melinda will want to dive again on my behalf," Roc said smoothly.

"Yes, she does," Melinda announced icily. "Melinda is just dying for you to make this claim. She would give her eyeteeth to find the ship and cram it—"

"Melly," her father interrupted her swiftly, "there's not a lot of time left."

"I don't want her doing it!" Roc said flatly. "I'm not going to leave my wife out here—"

"I'm not really your wife anymore."

"Yes, you damned well are."

"I will not—"

"Excuse us for just one minute, will you?" Roc suddenly demanded of the group. With an exasperated sigh, he suddenly grabbed Melinda and dived into the water.

Their combined weight sent them both deeply downward; then he kicked strongly to break the surface again.

Sputtering, Melinda stared at him furiously.

"Damn you!" she cried. "You already half-drowned me once today! What more—"

"It was the only way I could think of to have any privacy!"

"Trying to drown me again?"

"I didn't try to drown you. I just tried to get you alone for a few lousy minutes. You won't listen!"

"*I* won't listen! Oh, that's rich. I've begged and pleaded, I've made a fool of myself. I've been honest—"

"Yeah! Right after you crawled out of that net, right?"

She ignored that. "You haven't listened to me since I came aboard, not once, no matter what I said."

"I'm trying to tell you that I'm sorry."

"But it doesn't mean anything!"

"Damn it, Melinda, you made mistakes, I made mistakes, but the point is—"

"You've made a hell of a lot more of them recently than I have!"

"Yes!" he agreed. "Yes! I have."

"I'm going to my father's boat, as he suggested. I'm going to find that stinking *Contessa* for you. And then—"

"Then you'll talk to me, or I'll abandon the damn thing right now and let Eric Longford have it!"

Staring at him, seeing the passion, the fury, in his eyes, Melinda knew that he meant what he said. Her salt-laden lashes swept her cheeks. Maybe he was right; maybe they both had to put the past behind them.

"All right," she said softly. "We find the *Contessa*. Then we talk."

He reached a hand across the water in silent agreement.

"I can swim very well myself, thank you."

"I know," he told her, but he caught her hand anyway, and a few very powerful kicks brought them to the ladder at the bow of the *Crystal Lee*.

"I don't quite get this," Jonathan Davenport said, reaching down to help his daughter aboard, his eyes looking over her shoulder and focusing on Roc. "You've spent years talking about the *Contessa*. Months searching for her. Weeks on the brink of discovery. And now she's right beneath your damn feet, and the two of you are wasting time arguing!"

"We're not arguing," Roc said.

"We're discussing," Melinda grated out.

"And?"

"Roc's going to take the *Crystal Lee* in. I'm coming diving with you."

"Fine," Jonathan said in a determined voice. "Let's get going, then, eh? Eric's got divers in the water, and who knows, when you lead a horse to water, sometimes it does drink."

"Roc, Bruce and I are going to dive, too," Connie said quickly, still wearing a look of guilt and apology.

Roc sighed with exasperation, his shoulders slumping. "It's fine, Connie. It's fine."

"Roc—" Connie began.

"Connie, let's go," Melinda told her.

She stared at her husband one more moment, gritting her teeth, fighting tears and the wild urge to fly across the few feet between them and throw herself into his bronze arms.

Not now. Not now! She was still aching. . . .

She forced herself to turn away, but she could feel the heat of his stare as she climbed down the ladder to her father's dinghy.

Connie followed, then Bruce. Jonathan came last, picking up the oars, and sending them shooting across the water to his boat.

"Tanks!" Melinda said suddenly.

"You don't need to worry about a thing, I promise," her father told her.

"Melinda," Connie said suddenly, "I'm sorry. I'm so sorry."

"There's nothing for anyone to be sorry about at the moment. All's well that ends well, and we haven't finished this yet," Jonathan said.

"The *Contessa* is somewhere right beneath us," Bruce reminded them all quietly.

The oars slapped the water, and that was the only sound they heard as they finished the trip to Jonathan's boat. Jinks was there to help them aboard, waiting in the bow with diving tanks.

Her father had been awfully sure of himself, Melinda thought. And she almost smiled. Then a startling misery seemed to overwhelm her, right after

Jinks, tall, gnarled, as gentle as ever, gave her a welcoming hug.

She found herself suddenly in her father's arms, whispering softly, "He didn't believe me. He didn't trust me, Daddy,"

Jonathan lifted her chin, and she saw the tenderness and determination in his eyes.

"He's just a little raw, Melly. He thought his wounds had healed—and then they were all opened up again. But it's going to work out."

"How do you know?"

"Because he loves you."

She smiled, unable to say anything in reply.

"Jinks, help me with my tanks," she said instead. "Do you have my favorite flippers?"

"Yes, Melly, that I do," Jinks told her. In a few moments she was suited and ready, so she sat at the edge of the boat, waiting for Connie and Bruce. She stared out at the *Crystal Lee*. Any second now, she would disappear across the blue.

And Melinda was suddenly very determined that when she returned, she was going to have the *Contessa* on a platter to hand to Roc.

"There's something funny about this regulator," Jinks told Jonathan, frowning over Connie's equipment.

"Then get another one," Jonathan said. Melinda smiled at her father. Safety was one of his major concerns. Like Roc, he had often been angry with her for her recklessness. But it suddenly seemed as if everything was taking too much time. "I'm going down," she said.

"Melinda, Roc doesn't like you down alone," Bruce began.

"You'll be with me in minutes!" she assured him.

"Melinda!" her father called, but it was too late. She had already gone over, shooting through the depths, ending up right by the ledge.

The water was exceptionally beautiful. The afternoon sun was shining through, and the bright, stunning colors of the sea life surrounding the coral were vividly there before her. She saw the ledge and the edge of the World War Two wreck that had been intriguing her. She had found the casket wedged beneath it.

She swam deeper, studying the ledge, then caught hold of a rod protruding upward from the ship and tugged on it. At first nothing happened, so, in exasperation, she tugged again. It gave. Not a lot. Just an inch. She clenched her teeth and pulled again.

Suddenly it came free in her hand, and she went pitching backward with startling force. Sand spewed up all around her. There was a groaning sound as part of the World War Two wreck broke free and went tumbling, in slow motion, over the edge of the shelf.

Her heart hammered as she fought to maintain her position in the swirling waters. She saw a board sticking out from the bottom and she caught hold of it.

Slowly, the water around her began to settle. She stared at her hand, trembling inwardly.

Then she stared harder. She was holding on to a piece of lumber with a jagged tear beneath it. A very old piece of lumber. And now, with the piece of the other ship having fallen away, she went deeper, keeping her hand on the wood and tracing it to its source.

She nearly jumped. She'd come across a figurehead. The features were marred, eaten away by time. But there was a giant head before her, with long waving wooden hair.

Her heart slammed against her chest. She had found it. The *Contessa.*

The sun above her was suddenly blotted out. Frowning, she looked upward.

A boat was blocking the light above. No...it wasn't a boat blocking the sun, not alone. There was something else going on. It was hard to see. The water still hadn't really settled. It was churning, it was dark, it was...

It was *red!*

She swallowed hard, nearly losing control over her breathing, as she slowly realized just what was happening.

There was a boat above her. And the water was red.

The water was red because someone was chumming the water, throwing out gallon after gallon of blood and guts and dead fish and trying to summon every shark in the vicinity.

Even as she watched, the sharks began to move in, creating a frenzy of motion. She felt ill. She'd never been afraid of sharks in the water before—she kept her distance from them, and they kept their distance from her. She'd never done much diving in waters where great whites were prevalent, and she'd never seen one, though she had encountered lemons, blues, tigers and hammerheads. Sometimes they showed interest, and someone in the party would usually butt them away with a shark stick.

Most shark attacks, she knew, came when a shark was confused and thought that a person was his natural prey. It was one of the reasons there had been so many great white attacks off the coast of Northern California. The sharks looked up and saw the surfers' arms and legs paddling alongside their surfboards and thought they were sea lions, the creatures' customary diet.

She had never been afraid before, not really. But she was terrified now.

They weren't that far above her. Not forty-five feet. And there were more and more and more of them.... Some small, perhaps six feet.

Some larger... perhaps ten feet or so... And all of them thrashing, hideously thrashing, swimming in a frenzy, even snapping at one another.

She stared at them horrified. One swam downward in a sudden motion, then shot toward the food supply again. She edged against the body of the ship she had finally discovered.

Eric had discovered it, too, so it seemed. Or had been sure that she would.

Dear lord, she couldn't believe that someone she had known could want the treasure so badly that he would . . .

Murder her, she thought.

She had no defense against the sharks, none at all. And the water was growing bloodier by the second.

Eyes tearing, she fought the wild pull of desolation. It was so hard! All she could remember was wanting to run across the deck and throw herself into Roc's arms. She could remember the cobalt fire of his eyes. She could almost feel his warmth.

But she hadn't run to him, she had run away from him. She hadn't forgiven him. . . .

And now maybe it was going to be too late. He would come back and find the pieces of his *Contessa,* all right. And he would also find the pieces of his wife. . . .

She inhaled slowly, fighting desperately not to give way to fear. To hold on, to wait. She checked her watch. She needed to see how much time she had left in her air tanks.

Just then something bumped against her back with startling force, and in the bloodred depths of the water, she let loose a strangled scream.

Chapter 13

It was amazing how quickly things could change. One minute he was feeling the warmth of the late afternoon sun touching his shoulders as he cranked up the anchor, his heart weighted down by the fact that he might really have gone and done it this time.

Time had taught him that pride meant nothing in the darkness of the night. Well, he should have learned his lesson better. He had walked away once, so sure that he had been betrayed, so righteous.

Well, hell, maybe he had been right. It just didn't matter a lot. This time, he'd been wrong as hell. That just didn't matter, either.

He didn't think he would be able to bear it if he lost her a second time.

Those were his thoughts—about losing her—when he suddenly saw Jonathan waving frantically to him. "Hey, captain!" Peter called out at the same time. "Holy Mary! Look at the water!"

He did. He looked and saw a growing pool of blood in the water.

His heart jumped instantly to his throat.

At the same moment he noticed that the third boat—the uninvited boat, Eric Longford's boat—had already taken flight, skimming rapidly away over the water.

Panic seized him as his mind conjured up a terrible picture of a diver caught in the blades of a motor, ripped to shreds, bleeding....

Bruce? Connie?

Melinda?

Oh, God...

Then he realized that Jonathan had brought his own vessel to life, and the boat was nearing him at a dangerous pace. Finally, just in time to avoid a collision, the motor was cut. He could hear Jonathan shouting.

"That bastard! That damn *bastard!*"

"What in God's name?" Roc shouted to him.

"He chummed the water! The idiot must have found something, and he's trying to stake the first claim. Look at the damned water! And Melinda is down there!"

Once again Roc's heart slammed against his chest. Hard. A second ago he'd been afraid of losing her. Now they could all lose her—for good.

Steady, capable Jinks, who'd been with Jonathan for as long as Roc could remember, was pulling out gear. For a moment, staring at his father-in-law's face, Roc thought that Jonathan was going to jump in without tanks or mask, he was so desperate to reach his daughter.

"Wait!" Roc cried.

"There's no time to wait!" Jonathan cried back. "She only has an hour's worth of air. I've got—"

"You've got to pull your boat around over there, away from all the blood. I'm going down for her."

"I'm going—"

"Damn it, Jonathan, face it. I'm the fastest, and probably the best."

"She's my daughter!"

"She's my wife!"

"Eh, my friends!" Joe Tobago interrupted swiftly. "Whoever goes down first needs to be prepared. It seems to be a group of blues, though I think I saw a lemon or two. Nasty sharks. Mr. Davenport, if you take your boat around, I can pull the *Crystal Lee* into the middle of the swirl, shoot a few, and keep the others busy so that perhaps Cap'n Roc can bring your daughter up to you, eh?"

"It's the best way, Jonathan!" Roc shouted.

Peter had tanks, fins, a mask and regulator ready for Roc even as they spoke. He'd also brought a weight belt, with sheaths for two knives, and two shark sticks—six feet each, and primed to give a shark a good electric jolt when the point punched into the animal's tough flesh.

In all his years as a diver, Roc had used the electric prods only twice. He'd never been big on shark hunts; he'd always felt they had their place in the sea. Now he prayed that Peter could shoot the whole lot of them. There were plenty of big, sharp-toothed fish in the sea.

There was only one Melinda.

He got suited up amazingly swiftly, with Peter assuring him that he would have a solid hour's air to share with Melinda once he'd reached her.

Once. Peter stumbled over the word a little, almost saying *if* instead.

Well, if he couldn't reach her, it didn't matter. He didn't want to come up alone. He knew that now. No matter what the future held, he wouldn't come back without her.

"I'm going over!" he shouted to Jonathan. "Get your boat into position!"

"Get clear of the blood!" Jonathan shouted to him.

He was clear enough of it. He was afraid that if he didn't get down swiftly, he wouldn't find Melinda in time. He raised a hand in agreement, then sat on the edge of the *Crystal Lee* and let the weight of his tanks take him backward into the sea.

He splashed swiftly into the water, then sank into the once azure sea. He allowed the impetus of his fall to take him downward quickly, ten feet, twenty, thirty....

Then he stabilized himself. He could free dive deeper without causing himself any pressure difficulties, but the last thing he needed now was a case of the bends. Encumbered with gear as he was, he tried a slower drift to the ocean's depths.

Peter, he saw, was already at it with his gun. One of the sharks, a blue, about five and a half feet long, had been struck through the head with a bullet, pulling it and the frenzied throng around it away from Roc—and away from the ledge where Melinda had gone down.

For a moment he found himself watching the tempest with an awed fascination. It seemed that along with the blood and chunks of fish guts Longford had cast into the water, he had left some big bait, too, split tunas, good-sized groupers. The whole conglomeration was now floating around in a sea of blood, eerie, half eaten, sightless eyes staring about.

The sharks turned on the shot blue, whose nervous system had been hit. It thrashed and jerked wildly in the water, like a robot gone amok.

Roc drew his gaze from the tempest going on above him. The sharks—dear God, twenty of them? thirty?—hadn't paid him the least heed as yet. They were intent only on one thing—food. Within minutes the blue was half consumed, dinner for its kind before it had even succumbed to death.

Roc pulled his gaze from the tempest and looked to the shelf below. That was where Melinda had found the casket. It was where she would go to search for the lost ship.

He dived quickly, then thrust himself quickly backward as a large lemon shark came nosing into view. Smooth, slim, sleek, it was veering away from Roc, then made a sudden turn into him.

He hit it with the prod.

The shark shuddered and turned instantly away.

Roc blinked hard and turned toward the ledge again, reminding himself that he needed eyes in the back of his head. He kept seeing that wounded blue in his mind, thrashing wildly about, then bitten to pieces....

It couldn't have happened to Melinda. He wouldn't believe it. He wouldn't allow it to happen.

He reached the shelf and turned toward the crimson waters, trying to assure himself that no new predators were on their way toward him. The frenzy was still going on above him. As he watched, another shark went into a wild fit of thrashing, even farther away than the blue had been.

Peter had shot the creature, he was certain. And bit by bit, Peter was managing to draw the melee away from Roc.

And away from the shelf.

He pitched himself still more deeply downward, then saw the shelf loom into view. There was deep water to the left of it, he thought unwillingly. These were temperate waters. Makos, hammerheads and the like were known to frequent the area, though none of them had appeared as yet. And surely they were in far too temperate a zone for a great white to appear....

But they had appeared in these waters. Recently, actually.

He had to get a grip on himself. He had to find Melinda.

He swam swiftly alongside the shelf. Then, to his amazement, a wall of timber suddenly seemed to rise above him. He swam swiftly along it, certain that it had not been there before, that he had been to this exact spot and hadn't seen it.

He came upon a plaque. Grown over. Green with seaweed, laden down with barnacles. He ran a hand over it. Saw letters.

essa

He had found his ship, he realized.

A little late. Apparently Eric Longford had already found her, as had Melinda.

He shot down the length of the broken vessel, not giving a damn about it. He had to find Melinda. Panic began to set in as he realized that more and more sharks were congregating above, even if Peter was managing to move them somewhat.

He swam along the broken wooden bow. Ahead of him, he could see the outstretched, decaying arm of a figurehead. He swam hard toward it.

Suddenly he bumped into something coming around the edge of the ship.

And he saw, miraculously, that it was his wife.

She was about to scream. She had seen the sharks, of course. She had seen the tranquil azure waters become a pool of blood. And she had assumed that he was one of the beasts.

The underwater world was known to be silent. It wasn't entirely true. He could hear her scream.

And around his mouthpiece, he shouted to her in turn. "It's me! Careful. Careful!"

Her eyes were very wide, terrified. Well, hell, he had felt that way himself. Yet at the sight of him, she seemed to feel better. She threw her arms around him, clinging to him.

He drew her closer. Held her there for a moment, trembling inside as he realized that while she was alive there was hope.

They had a chance.

But that didn't change the fact that there was a feeding frenzy going on directly above them, that other predators of the deep were hurrying to join in the tempest.

He realized suddenly that she was nearly out of air. He motioned for her to spit out her mouthpiece and take his. Then he shouted to her in the water. It would be just possible for her to make out his words if she tried.

"We've got to head north! To your father's boat. Do you understand?"

She nodded gravely.

He thrust one of the shark sticks into her grasp, then took the mouthpiece back, just as he was about to inhale sea water.

"Your tanks are no good. We have to share. Understand?"

Again, she nodded, then took a breath from his regulator before trying to talk to him. "Roc! It's the *Contessa!*"

"I know, I know. But we've got to get out of here."

She nodded. She did know. But she suddenly let the mouthpiece float between them for a moment so her lips could touch his.

She mouthed the words, *Roc. I love you! You came for me.*

He mouthed back to her, *I'd come for you anywhere!*

He set the mouthpiece between her lips, forcing her to inhale deeply. Then he took another breath himself and indicated the length of the hull of the *Contessa.* She nodded her understanding.

Slowly, carefully, they started down the length of it.

Halfway down, Roc spotted a curious blue. It was only about seven feet long, but it came very near them, fascinated by the call of the blood in the water.

He was ready, prodding the animal swiftly. It shuddered violently and moved off.

It wasn't big, Roc knew. Not by shark standards. But that didn't matter. It had rows of fantastically sharp teeth, and one bite from it . . .

Would have brought on a hundred more!

They were past it, though. Past it. No matter what happened, he couldn't give way to panic.

He reminded himself that there were researchers who purposely baited the water, anxious to study the creatures. Film crews sometimes went among them, filming events such as this. They survived because they kept cool heads.

And a cool head was what they needed now.

They moved slowly along the length of the ship.

How odd, he thought. After all this time, they had found the *Contessa.* And they were using her to make their escape from the tempest in the sea above them.

She was long, one hundred and fifty feet. She was also badly damaged. There really wasn't all that much left. A broken up hull, long covered by the wreck of a World War Two ship. The last vessel had fallen almost completely over the first one. Both of them victims of the sea.

Well, he was determined that they would not be victims, too.

He tried to peer through the water. It wasn't nearly as crimson here as it had been at the figurehead. If he looked ahead, he was certain he could see the outline of Jonathan Davenport's ship. But to reach it, they would have to leave the comparative safety of the decaying hulk of the *Contessa.*

He paused, forcing Melinda to take a deep draft of air. Then he indicated the ship, and she nodded. He pointed to her shark stick, and she nodded again. They had dived together so often before. Even now, Roc thought, they were a good team.

Back to back, they began a northward ascent.

A curious lemon, a small one, came unnervingly close. Roc prodded it. The shark veered away, but it didn't leave.

A second later another shark began milling uncomfortably close. A blue this time.

Then another blue. And another lemon. Circling them. Swimming away, coming back in again. Close.

Too close.

Too many sharks for them to prod off at one time.

Melinda seemed to sense his thoughts. She turned into him suddenly, taking air from him, then letting the mouthpiece fall. With the sea beasts all around him, she threw her arms around him again— And kissed him.

One last kiss.

Just then Roc felt a sudden thrust against his body. He waited for the rip of teeth, thinking that perhaps he could thrust Melinda upward if the creature had him. But he felt nothing.

Then again, he had heard that a shark bite was so swift and sharp that divers often didn't feel the teeth.

He looked down, expecting half of his leg to be gone. But his leg wasn't gone at all. And the sharks were backing away. Even in the midst of their frenzy, they were backing away.

Because Hambone had come.

The playful dolphin was beneath them now, circling slowly, then suddenly streaking through the water and butting against one of the sharks, which seemed to flop away through the water.

Hambone swam back to them, and Roc caught a firm hold on the dolphin's flipper. They began to move swiftly. He clung to the flipper and Melinda clung to him.

Miraculously Hambone brought them through the water as if they were flying, somehow knowing that they needed to go north.

Past the field of blood, ten feet from Melinda's father's boat, Roc released his hold on the dolphin's flipper. Moments later they broke the surface, not five feet from the boat.

"Thank you, God!" they heard suddenly.

Roc, spitting out his mouthpiece, looked up. Jonathan was at the edge of the boat, looking very old at that moment, and reaching down to help his daughter aboard.

"Melinda!" he shouted to her.

"Dad!" she cried back.

But she didn't take his hand, not right away. She ripped off her mask and stared at Roc. "Hambone!" she cried, then dived under.

Roc instantly followed his wife.

The dolphin had come back to them, swimming beneath Melinda, allowing her to stroke his back. To say thank you.

Roc reached out and touched the dolphin, too, staring into the dark eye of the gentle beast, trying to mentally communicate his own appreciation. Then he clamped a hand on his wife's wrist. They could thank Hambone further later. It was time for the two of them to get aboard.

A hard kick propelled them to the surface once again, and Jonathan was ready once again. He reached down and grabbed his daughter. Bruce and Connie were there, ready too, to pull Roc from the sea. In seconds he and Melinda were both free of their gear, encompassed in warm terry towels and holding steaming cups of coffee.

"You made it. You made it!" Jonathan said anxiously. "Thank God!"

"Thanks Roc," Melinda said, her smile beautiful as she glanced his way.

He couldn't take credit. Not under the circumstances. "Thanks to a dolphin!" he said softly.

"Thanks to anything!" Jonathan cried. "You weren't touched?" he said to his daughter. "Scratched, harmed—"

"Dad, I'm fine." She looked at her husband again. "I knew I'd be fine the moment I saw Roc's face."

She frowned suddenly and stood. Her towel fell from her shoulders, and she thrust her coffee cup to Bruce as she said, "Oh, my God. Roc! You came back for me! That idiot who nearly murdered us both is going to manage to make the claim on your *Contessa!*"

Roc stood, His towel fell, too. Then he thrust *his* coffee cup into Bruce's hands as he caught her in his arms, lifting her chin.

"Who gives a damn about the *Contessa!*" he told her. "Your father told me something once, the truest words I've ever heard. I could search the sea forever, but it wouldn't matter. I've found my treasure. If you'll just forgive me for being a doubting bastard, I swear I will never forget again that I have the greatest treasure a man can find—my wife."

There was silence on the boat. The dying sun was golden and orange, its rays streaking across the heavens and the seas. Then Melinda spoke at last. "Oh, my God! Roc, that was beautiful."

"Can we start out fresh?" he asked very softly.

"Yes!" she whispered. "Oh, yes!"

He kissed her. Kissed her as the last rays of the sun touched them. Kissed her until Jonathan cleared his throat at last.

"Well, that's lovely, you two, just lovely. But I might be able to add a wee touch of icing to the cake here."

Roc, his arms around Melinda, turned to his father-in-law. "And what's that, Jonathan?"

"Well, the *Contessa is* yours, my boy."

Roc arched a brow. "Jonathan, even if we tried to convince the authorities that Eric was willing to commit murder to stake his claim, we'd have one hell of a time proving it. In another hour, there won't be much sign of what happened here."

Jonathan smiled smugly, taking a seat on the rail. "But you see, that slimy bastard is going to make it into port to discover that a firm claim has already been made on the *Contessa.*"

"*You* made a claim?" Melinda gasped.

Jonathan shook his head. Then he nodded. "Well, yes. And no," he said.

"You've gone and outdone me again," Roc said, but there was no anger in his words.

Jonathan shook his head firmly. "I made the claim, all right, Roc. But I did it in your name. I just happened to get lucky the day my daughter opted out on me and managed to get that slime to drop her off in the middle of the ocean. I made the same find Melinda did, a few pieces of silverware." He shrugged. "I hadn't actually found the ship, but...well, hell, it had to be here. So I made the claim, saying that I was in your employ for the time."

Roc stared at his father-in-law. Then he threw up his hands. "But if you made the find—"

"I didn't make the find! I still thought you were an idiot about the whole thing, but then, the last time I'd doubted you, well, I was proved a fool. In many, many ways," he added softly.

"But, Jonathan—"

"Roc, the find is yours. It always was. And there wouldn't be a damned bit of justice in the world if you didn't accept me as a crew member on this one."

Roc had gone stiff. Melinda could feel it.

"I don't know, Jonathan. Thinking is one thing. Finding is another."

But Jonathan stretched out a hand to his son-in-law. "I have a feeling we might be working together again—son."

"You taught me so much. This—"

"And you've managed to teach me a hell of a lot, too. How about it, Cap'n Trellyn?"

Melinda wanted to cry out loud in frustration as Roc continued to stand so stiffly. He was so proud.

Then she felt it. Felt the give within him, the massive release of tension. And he stretched out his hand to her father.

"Deal?" Jonathan said softly.

"Deal," Roc agreed.

"Wow!" Melinda cried.

She kissed her husband again, then her father, and then Bruce and Connie and Jinks.

And by then the *Crystal Lee* had come alongside them again, and it was agreed that Roc's boat was probably better equipped for the kind of celebration they had in mind for that evening. Jonathan's boat was left at anchor, and even gnarled old Jinks came aboard the *Crystal Lee.*

Within seconds the rest of the crew heard the news about the claim—no matter what Eric had done. Soon a bottle of champagne had been popped open, and everyone was kissing everyone.

Then Roc said with a determined purpose that he and Melinda were going to shower and change. The others nodded and lifted their glasses to them.

Melinda thought her father's eyes were sparkling, but she didn't really get a chance to see for sure. Roc was propelling her to his cabin. In a minute the door was closed behind them, and just seconds after that she found herself in his arms.

Feeling his kiss. The wild heat of his breath. The fire of his body.

"My God!" he whispered. "I was so scared. So damn scared. I thought I'd really lost you."

"You came for me!" she whispered. "Through sharks, through blood..."

He pulled away from her suddenly. "Does that mean you'll stay married to me?"

She drew in her breath swiftly and nodded, beautiful eyes on his. "As long as it means *you* don't intend to divorce *me,*" she said softly.

"Never," he promised. "Like I said before," he added huskily, "I've found my real treasure."

"Oh, Roc," she whispered as he swept her into his arms, carrying her to the bunk, "that really is beautiful."

He smiled, stretching her out then lying down beside her and tugging away the strap of her bathing suit so he could place a searing, sensual kiss on her shoulder.

"You are more precious than any treasure in the sea," he assured her. Then his lips found hers. When they broke away, he asked softly, "Forgive me?"

"Oh, God, yes!" she cried.

"Then I have everything I could ever want!" he told her.

She wound her arms around him. Felt his kiss again. His touch. Erotic, sweet...

He stripped away her suit, and she shivered, trembled, wanted him.

After all, they had life. And they had each other. But...

"Roc, we told my father we'd be right out—"

He laughed huskily, cobalt eyes touching hers. "Your father isn't expecting us any time soon."

"But the rest of the crew—"

"Well, I imagine they'll all think we're making mad, passionate love in my cabin."

"And—"

"And!" he said, placing a finger on her lips to still her words. "That's exactly what we're going to be doing."

He lifted his finger. She smiled slowly.

"Anything to say?" he asked her.

"Umm," she murmured.

"Well?"

"Let's get to the mad, passionate part!" she told him, winding her arms around him.

He proceeded to do so.

Epilogue

"How beautiful!" Melinda cried softly, looking out across the white-tipped waves.

It was a rough day; storm clouds were threatening. There weren't many people on the whale watch that had left from Plymouth Harbor that afternoon; the weather had steered them away. But it hadn't seemed so awful to Roc and Melinda.

It had taken them months to rescue the *Contessa*'s treasures from the sea, and they had been good months. Melinda would always be eternally grateful for them. Her father had worked with them hand in hand, and there had been a bond forged between them that could never be broken now.

She was happy. She had never thought she could be so happy.

Yet no matter how well work had gone, Roc had been determined that they were going to take a trip away for their fifth anniversary. He was determined to really celebrate the event—even if they had been apart for three of their married years.

He had decided they were going to do something different, so they had left their customary warm climate to spend a few weeks in a cool New England fall.

But they hadn't quite managed to leave the sea behind. Roc had suggested the whale watch, and since Melinda considered even the big humpbacks to be close relations to Hambone, she had readily agreed.

"Thar she blows!" someone called.

Everyone came rushing over to the rail to see the spectacular creature.

The humpback descended, and Roc turned his attention to Melinda. "Did you read Connie's letter yet?" he asked her suddenly.

She shook her head. This seemed like a good time, while they waited for another whale to surface. She drew the letter from her leather handbag and ripped it open. Roc studied her features.

"What?"

"Why—how could they!" Melinda exploded.

"What?" Roc repeated.

Melinda stared at him, eyes full of both anger and amusement.

"They eloped!"

"Connie and—"

"My father!"

"Well, we can hardly be shocked," Roc advised her. "There's definitely been something going on between those two for a long time now."

"I know that, but why would they elope...? I mean, we should have been there!"

"Your father isn't exactly a spring chicken," Roc said.

"But still, you'd think he'd want us there—oh!"

She had kept reading. Now she stared at Roc again.

"What?"

She started to giggle. "They, er, had to elope. Roc, I'm going to have a sibling!"

"Sibling?"

"They're having a baby—Connie's pregnant!"

Roc sat back and started to laugh. "Well, well."

Melinda stared thoughtfully at the letter. "Hmm. That makes Connie your stepmother-in-law."

"I suppose so."

"But now... my father will be our baby's grandfather, and Connie will be a mother with a step-grandchild and I wonder what our—"

"Our what?" Roc demanded.

Melinda stared at him. Then she smiled slowly. "Our baby. We're, uh, we're having one, too. I didn't really discuss it with you, but then, I didn't really plan it." He was still staring at her. She sighed. "It's what happens when you make mad passionate love in a cabin."

He finally started to laugh. Then he said, "Really?" She nodded, and he swept her into his arms, cradled her chin in his hands and kissed her.

"There! Over there! Thar she blows gain!" someone called.

But neither of them paid the least bit of attention. Roc just kept kissing her.

And when his lips parted from hers, she whispered happily, "I wonder if it will be a boy or a girl."

He held her chin again and met her eyes. "It won't matter in the least. Because there's one thing I know it will be."

She arched a brow at him.

"A treasure," he said softly. And he smiled. "A treasure from the sea!"

She smiled again, then kissed him.

* * * * *

COMING NEXT MONTH

HELL ON WHEELS
Naomi Horton

He Who Dares

Trucker Shay McKittrick had just stopped for a quick meal, but he came away from the café with a terrified, half-frozen stowaway desperate to make a fast getaway. Was this mystery woman really in danger?

NO EASY WAY OUT
Paula Detmer Riggs

Journalist Arden Crawford thought there was something familiar about Dylan Kincade. What terrible secret could he be hiding? Nothing could change the way she was feeling...could it?

COMING NEXT MONTH

IRONHEART
Rachel Lee

Under Blue Wyoming Skies

Gideon Ironheart could tell that Sara Jane Yates was a black satin sheets woman hiding out in the guise of a Deputy Sheriff. She was woman enough to make him think about settling down…

WADE CONNER'S REVENGE
Julia Quinn

Wade Conner had come back and another little girl had gone missing. It was up to Leigh Hampton and the man she'd always loved to find the scared child because the rest of town suspected Wade.

COMING NEXT MONTH FROM

Intrigue

Danger, deception and desire—
new from Silhouette...

NEVER SAY DIE Tess Gerritsen
DEEP IN THE BAYOU Joanna Wayne
IN SELF DEFENCE Saranne Dawson
MOON WATCH Vickie York

Special Edition

Satisfying romances packed with emotion

MAIL ORDER COWBOY Patricia Coughlin
B IS FOR BABY Lisa Jackson
THE GREATEST GIFT OF ALL Penny Richards
WHEN MORNING COMES Christine Flynn
COWBOY'S KIN Victoria Pade
LET'S MAKE IT LEGAL Trisha Alexander

Desire

Provocative, sensual love stories for the
woman of today

THE ACCIDENTAL BRIDEGROOM Ann Major
TWO HEARTS, SLIGHTLY USED Dixie Browning
THE BRIDE SAYS NO Cait London
SORRY, THE BRIDE HAS ESCAPED Raye Morgan
A GROOM FOR RED RIDING HOOD Jennifer Greene
BRIDAL BLUES Cathie Linz